DARLENE LUNSFORD

LAND OF PROMISE

by Darlene Lunsford

Editor: Cynthia Hickey
Book Design by Winged Publications

ISBN-13: 978-1-959788-79-9

In memory of my first husband Dave (Delaney), who shared a memorable year in Venezuela with me as well as numerous other adventures before he died. And who always encouraged my writing.

Also, to my dear Luns (Dave Lunsford), my husband of two years and four months, who loves me in all my craziness, is my best friend, and who supports me in all my personal endeavors. Though we've already been to 15 states and two countries together in our short married life, I look forward to many more travels with you!

Last but not least -- a heartfelt thanks to my family and friends who continue to be there for me through thick and thin!

"Delight yourself also in the Lord, and He will give you the desires of your heart." Ps. 37:4

CHAPTER ONE

Arrival in a New Country

K aren fought back tears as the plane taxied the runway. Her excitement of the last three months while preparing for a year in Venezuela was overshadowed by the anxieties mounting in her. As the plane lifted up, leaving Florida and heading for South America, her heart was heavy. Right now, all she wanted was to turn the plane around and go back to her own safe little corner of the world.

Her eyes focused politely on the flight attendant demonstrating safety procedures, but her mind was back in Seattle. At the prospect of serving as head cook in a school for missionary children, she had quit her job as legal assistant at the law firm. *Had* she been out of her mind then, as some of the more outspoken ones had accused? How could she just *leave*? At the time, there had been no doubt. Even throughout the next couple of months, while presenting her plans to different churches and small groups for raising the year's support, not once had she doubted her decision. Only now, alone and more than a little afraid, did she wonder.

What disturbed her most, though, was her boyfriend's reaction to the whole thing. "Karen, are you out of your MIND?" Jeff had shouted. "Do you expect me to wait around a whole year while you run around South America?"

Shocked, Karen had desperately attempted to maintain her composure. "It's just something I have to do," she had quietly explained. "I know it in my heart."

"Has your heart also told you what *I'm* supposed to do all year?" he had asked. Then, softening, he kissed her gently and pleaded, "Karen, I love you--*please* don't go...."

Tears running down her cheeks at the memory, she pushed a strand of blonde hair away from her forehead. What bothered her more than Jeff not waiting was the fact that she had been so *wrong* about him. From the beginning of their relationship, she thought he held the same values as herself. He had allowed her to believe so--but she had been wrong in believing he put God first. When it was convenient, *maybe*. But when it came to self-sacrificing for the Lord, Jeff wanted only what was best for Jeff.

Karen sat back in her seat and closed her eyes. Though usually eager to meet new people, for the moment she was grateful for the empty seat beside her, letting her tears fall unabashed. She had come knowing

Jeff wouldn't wait. Now only God could fill the emptiness in her heart.

As the motion sickness pills began to take effect, Karen gratefully felt herself being lulled to sleep. Her thoughts were of people and places she knew well, and for a short time she was back in Seattle in the heart of the busy city.

She awoke, feeling rested, just as the plane was beginning its descent. Her heart gave a leap. This was Venezuela, her first taste of South America. The past was behind her now. This was her new home, her new land, for almost a whole year. Karen hoped she could remember enough high school Spanish to get through customs and prayed that Mr. Birch, the principal from the academy, would be at the airport to meet her.

After stepping off the plane, her eyes quickly searched the waiting area. Having never met Mr. Birch before, she had no idea how to recognize him. Anxiously she scanned the crowd for a single white face among the brown-skinned Venezuelans.

To her great relief, a hand waved wildly behind the thick glass window that separated the newcomers from the waiting crowd. She smiled and waved back to the white male face peering at her, then fell into a line to wait for her suitcases. After what seemed an eternity, her two large floral bags appeared on the conveyer belt. Setting her small bag down for a minute, Karen lifted the large suitcases onto the floor.

Struggling to carry all three pieces of luggage, Karen was taken aback as two men approached, one pulling on each large bag. "No--" she cried and shook her head. They looked puzzled and rattled off a few words in Spanish to her. "No--*gracias*," she said, and they reluctantly put down the luggage. Maybe they were just trying to be helpful, but in any case she did not want them running off with her things.

She again picked up the bags and joined the line to go through customs. As she waited, a young boy approached, pointing to her suitcases. "No." Karen shook her head firmly. She certainly did not want help from strangers. If she needed help, she was certain the man from the school would assist. Karen wished he could be here now, as she had reached the head of the line and two male customs agents were looking at her and asking questions in rapid Spanish. Karen shook her head helplessly. They shrugged and opened her suitcases.

"What are you doing?" she protested, then remembered all she had heard about the cautious scrutiny of everything that came into the country. So she patiently waited, hot, tired, and a little embarrassed at them going through her personal belongings, until all three bags had been searched and zipped shut. At long last they stamped the seal of approval on her passport and waved her on through the glass door where a large group of people waited.

A man with graying hair and a salt-and-pepper mustache immediately pushed his way forward and took her hand. "I'm Paul Birch, the principal," he said, his blue eyes twinkling. "Welcome to Venezuela!"

She smiled, relieved at his friendly presence, and heartily shook the outstretched hand. "Hi, I'm Karen. And I'm *very* glad to see you!" Glancing behind her, she asked, "What do these men want, anyway?" Two different Venezuelans were following her.

"They want to carry your luggage--but I think the two of us can manage." He spoke a few words of Spanish and the men reluctantly left. "With your blonde hair and white skin, you're attracting the nationals like a magnet!"

Karen looked at him, puzzled.

"South Americans think all North Americans are rich," he explained as they walked down the hallway to the exit. "After all, think of how much of their money it would take to even *get* here from the States! Those men make a full-time living by carrying bags--what an American tips them would likely cut their workday in half!"

Smothering heat enveloped Karen the moment Mr. Birch opened the wide double doors to the outside world. Perspiration beaded on her forehead and upper lip. "Whew!" she gasped and paused to catch her breath. "Is it always this bad?"

"No--sometimes it's worse!" Mr. Birch quipped, laughing. "You get used to it. Actually, though, this does seem to be one of our hotter days." He loaded the luggage in the trunk and drove out of the airport.

"Going through customs can be a harrowing experience," he told her. "At least your suitcases weren't packed so tightly that you had to totally repack them after inspection!"

"Do they always go through all the bags?"

"They're supposed to. Although, I have seen them just wave a person on. It all depends. You can *buy* your way through, but we don't recommend it. Besides, then it looks as though you've something to hide."

"What are they looking for?" Karen asked innocently, grateful that the vehicle's air-conditioning was beginning to circulate cool air.

"Drugs, mostly. And if you bring anything valuable expensive in, they'll make you pay duty on it. Sometimes as much as a couple hundred dollars."

They drove in silence for a minute or two. Karen glanced over at her driver. Mr. Birch seemed cool enough in gray slacks and a short-sleeved cotton shirt, but she couldn't help wondering why he wasn't in shorts. Gathering a little courage, she broached the subject. "I notice that you're wearing long pants in this heat," she said. "Do you always have to dress up because you're the principal?"

Mr. Birch did not seem to take offense at her question. "If you'll notice, not even the Venezuelans are wearing shorts, except the children. Shorts aren't really the custom here," he explained. "I hope it doesn't cramp your style, but we're fairly strict with the staff. For sports we allow them, if they're modest--even for the guys--but for anything off-campus the students and staff are required to wear long pants or dresses."

"Oh." Karen hoped what she was wearing was appropriate. Knowing she would be in muggy weather all day, she had chosen for her traveling outfit a white knit shirt with tan capris cut mid-calf.

"Your own outfit is fine, if you're wondering," Mr. Birch informed Karen as if reading her thoughts. He glanced over at her.

Relieved, she smiled. "Good. I *was* wondering." Karen was nervous as they traveled along the winding mountain roads. She noted how Mr. Birch drove with caution but also aggressively passed when necessary and slowed down for others passing on the mountain curves. She tensed.

"Do they always drive like this?"

Mr. Birch chuckled. "Welcome to South America! I always forget what it's like for a new person. This is nothing. The only way to survive here is to drive like they do. And it's completely the opposite of the defensive driving we learn in the States."

Karen leaned back against the vinyl seat and tried to relax, taking in the sights around her. Boys threw rocks across the road, women sat talking and snapping green beans, men carried bananas to waiting trucks. Chickens ran loose in the yards. A boy sold watermelons from a roadside stand. Far in the distance a mountain range stretched from one end of the sky to the other.

"I'm really here, aren't I?" she said with a touch of homesickness.

Mr. Birch didn't seem to notice the lonely tone in her voice. "Yes, and we're certainly glad you are! My wife Lois has worked in the kitchen before, but she wasn't looking forward to filling in for a whole school year. So, when we found out you were coming--let me tell you, you are a real answer to prayer."

Karen's heart leaped. "An answer to prayer?" she repeated out loud. It *was* right to come here, and if she hadn't fully realized it before, she did now. Karen let the words sink in. *She was an answer to prayer.*

"Yes, we've been praying for a new head cook at Wednesday evening prayer meeting for weeks," Mr. Birch told her. "Of course, Rob will help too. And the kitchen maids."

"Rob?"

"The food buyer. Grocery shopping is a job in itself, and one for someone fluent in Spanish, so of course, we don't expect you to do it. Although you may want to go along once in a while just to get an idea of what foods are available. Rob helped in the kitchen last year, so he can show you the ropes. He also teaches a couple of computer classes. You'll find him very helpful--he's familiar with the language and can tackle just about anything that comes up. He understands the budget, too, and will help you get a handle on that."

"So, the shopping isn't as easy as going to the supermarket, I take it?" Karen asked.

He grinned. "Not at all. Rob might end up going to as many as ten places for ten different things. But it's not usually so bad. Fresh vegetables and fruits he gets at Friday market. Whipped cream we buy over the border in Columbia, when someone is going on a shopping trip anyway. Chickens and eggs are delivered from a nearby farm. Some things can be purchased at the local store, but we also make a lot ourselves--all our own bread, salad dressings, syrup. When oranges are at a good price, the maids even make fresh juice. Señor Mantilla, the school's gardener, grows green beans and squash in a big patch out back."

Karen nodded, then let out a heavy sigh. "It all sounds a little overwhelming at the moment. I'm a bit worn out from the flight."

Mr. Birch smiled at her. "Don't worry--this first week will be pretty much just adjusting to all the changes and getting to know everyone. We'll give you all the time you need and there is a lot of help available. We're blessed with a truly wonderful staff. Some of the most dedicated Christians I know."

Karen held in her breath as they went around a sharp curve, then noticed a curious sight on the side of the road. "What's that?" she asked, pointing to what appeared to be a shrine set just off the pavement.

"Oh--that means someone has died there. Every time a person dies in a car accident, the family and friends put up a cross, sometimes more, in memory of that person. On some corners there are several."

Karen nodded. "I've seen that done in the States, but not often."

"Here it's almost a ritual," explained Mr. Birch. "They pray and place a rock at the base of the cross...if the prayer is answered, then the news travels fast. Crosses are nearly buried in rocks sometimes because people are hoping the person will help them get their prayers answered."

Karen was silent for a moment, then commented aloud, "How sad that people believe that a dead human being can help them get their prayers answered!"

Mr. Birch nodded solemnly. "Exactly. But that's what their religion teaches. Only one of many false notions that we as Christian believers are trying to combat. Even after a person accepts Christ here, though, it's difficult for them to put aside all their old traditional ways and simply put their faith in God."

They chatted amicably a while longer. Mr. Birch slowed the car as they drove into a small town, which he announced as Rubio. Karen noted the houses, most made of brick or stucco, with barred windows and tiled rooftops, each surrounded by a wrought iron fence with a locked gate. One even had a protective wall of cement blocks, with sharp pieces of broken glass sticking out along the top edge.

"So, this is Rubio," she mused. "Why do the homes all have metal fences and gates and bars across the windows?"

"There's a lot of robbery in Venezuela," Mr. Birch explained. "Most people have guard dogs, too. Including the school."

"Oh no, LOOK!" Karen squealed, sitting up in her seat. There, up ahead, was a large brown and white cow walking in the middle of the dusty street. "Should we go help put it back in?"

Mr. Birch laughed. "I'm afraid it *is* 'in'. During the day there are several that wander around wherever they please, but at night they go home on their own. Another one of our cultural delights."

Karen's mouth dropped open. "Are you serious?"

He laughed again, then pointed out the window. "There's the boys' dorm on the right....see, it has a ten-foot fence around it. And here's the school and the girls' dorm." He pulled into a long driveway and drove up in front of a red brick building bearing the name "Naughton Hall." Several deck chairs sat near the entrance, and a large, dark German Shepherd lay sprawled across the doorway.

"Naughton Hall houses the junior and senior girls' dorms," he continued, "as well as the dining hall, kitchen, laundry room, and two apartments, one of which is yours. The other is used for storage at the moment." He opened the trunk for Karen's suitcases and together they carried them to the door. Karen was amused that the dog opened one eye but gave no hint of leaving his select spot in front of the door.

"Move, Yogi," ordered Mr. Birch.

When the dog did not respond, Karen laughed. "Do YOU own this place?" she asked the dog, gently tousling his ear. Mr. Birch gave him a nudge with his foot. Yogi stood and began to wag his tail as Karen continued to pet him.

"He doesn't look very ferocious!" Karen said.

Mr. Birch gave Yogi an affectionate scratch on the head. "That's because you're white-skinned. Believe it or not, he doesn't ever bark at North Americans. But he barks and growls at just about every Venezuelan that comes in here, including the delivery men! Some of whom have been coming here for years!"

Just inside the wide double doors, Mr. Birch set down the bags.

Karen said, "See ya later, Yogi," and trailed along behind.

"This is the *sala*," he told her, "the gathering place, or living room. There is the dining hall--as you can see, we can accommodate up to 240 people at a time."

Karen glanced around. The dining hall was wall to wall with long tables, and a piano sat in one corner of the room. Colorful green and yellow paisley curtains that would have been considered old-fashioned in the States hung proudly from the tall windows on two sides of the building. As Mr. Birch led Karen into the kitchen, they were greeted by two smiling Venezuelan maids lifting pans of fresh hamburger buns out of the oven.

"Hello," Mr. Birch greeted them both. "This is Lucy," he told Karen, indicating a young Venezuelan maid wearing a cotton dress covered by a flour-dusted apron. "She's especially good at baking bread, cinnamon rolls, even English muffins." The maid, a beautiful girl with flashing dark eyes, long dark hair, and a bright smile, responded with a few shy words in Spanish. "And this is Rosalba," Mr. Birch went on. The older maid smiled, and Karen took an immediate liking to her. She had the weathered look of one who worked hard but kept her good humor. Karen smiled back, uncertain what to say from her limited Spanish vocabulary. "*Mucho gusto*," she said awkwardly.

The kitchen featured several long counters on which to work, large metal bins for flour and sugar, a pantry, three gas stoves, and a large walk-in refrigerator and freezer. The cupboards held thick glass dishes and cups. Shelves were full of pots, pans, and trays. Karen stood quietly taking it all in.

Mr. Birch read her thoughts. "Pretty impressive, isn't it?" He walked over and showed her the commercial-sized KitchenAid for mixing bread dough and cookies and mashing potatoes. "The kitchen is very self-contained. It has just about everything you'll need. No microwave yet, but Roxie has one upstairs in the dorm if you want to borrow one occasionally."

Karen nodded. "It's just--it's all... a little overwhelming," she told him again. "I feel so...inadequate." Then she laughed. "I guess that's not exactly the right thing to say to one's new boss, is it?"

He smiled understandingly. "That's how everyone feels at first. If you weren't right for the position, you'd never have made it this far. Are you a cook for a school back home?"

Karen laughed nervously. "No, that's the funny part--I'm a legal assistant. I had really hoped to come to the field and work in the office, but the mission representative says the same secretary has been here for years and there was no need in that area. So, he asked me to consider being head cook.

"The idea struck me as odd at first," Karen continued. "I mean, I don't even cook much at home! But the representative stressed that very little of the job was actually cooking. He needed someone who was a team player, organized, efficient and flexible, someone who is good at giving directions as well as taking constructive criticism." At this point she gave Mr. Birch a bright smile. "After hearing that, I felt I shouldn't rule it out. So here I am."

Mr. Birch returned her smile. "And we're very glad you are. In a sense, we're all in the same boat, Karen. We're all here for God to use--don't worry, no one's looking for perfection." He paused, then said in a quiet, even tone, "Sometimes God sends people to do a job, and while they're doing that job they find out why He really wanted them here. Just be ready for whatever God has in store for you."

His last comment left Karen a little flustered, but he quickly moved on to the next area. After a quick tour of the laundry room and an introduction to Carmen, the laundry maid, they walked upstairs to view the girls' dorm and meet Joe and Roxie, the junior girls' dorm parents. Joe, a New Yorker with the accent to match, shook hands with her heartily. His wife Roxie, with layered light brown hair and a friendly smile, assured Karen how glad she was that Karen had come, and offered to help in any way she could. "Or, if you just need to talk," she told Karen, "I'm here. I know it's always hard the first few months. Even the first week!"

Karen was grateful for the offer. "When will I meet everyone else?" she asked Mr. Birch as they walked back downstairs.

"Probably not until tonight at the picnic. Every Saturday all the teachers, staff, and students get together for supper. Since school's not in session yet, tonight it's just teachers and staff and their families, but usually there are around a hundred of us."

"Wow! *Every* Saturday night?"

"Hmm hmm. Six o'clock sharp. Everyone really looks forward to it. Out front at the barbecue pit." He continued in a businesslike tone. "I've arranged for you to take meals in staff homes tomorrow--I'll make sure you meet the families tonight and you can arrange times to be picked up. You'll start work on Monday. Sorry I can't give you more of a break than that, but with students arriving next week we need you to be trained as soon as possible. My wife will help the first week, but we have two small children, and she teaches a Spanish class, so she'll be glad when you feel ready to take the lead. After that it will just be you and Rob. You'll be in charge of the kitchen, but don't underestimate Rob's help. He'll do breakfast with you, since the maids don't arrive until eight, and he'll help with supper. And weekends, since the maids leave early on Saturday and are off on Sunday."

He continued. "If there is a dispute, you'll make the final decision, and if there's a problem too big for both of you, come talk to me about it. I don't expect any major problems, though--and somehow I can't imagine you and Rob not getting along." His eyes twinkled and his moustache twitched into a smile.

Karen, suddenly realizing she was exhausted, asked to be shown to her apartment. Remembering her bags, they walked back to the front entrance to retrieve them. Mr. Birch opened her door with a key, then gave the key to Karen and told her he would see her at the picnic. Karen thanked him and stepped inside.

Alone, she surveyed her surroundings. The apartment, located just across from the school's kitchen, was small but cozy. A little refrigerator, stove, and a long counter comprised the kitchen on one side of the large room. A maroon-flowered sofa graced one wall, with wicker chairs on either side, a wicker and glass coffee table, and a few large potted plants. The bedroom had a bed, a desk, bookshelves, and a built-in dresser. The tiny bathroom was standard, except for a large tiled shower instead of a tub. "Really quite modern," she mused. But what had she expected--a mud hut with a thatched roof? After taking a quick look around, she collapsed onto the bed and slept soundly.

The sound of metal pans clanging across the hall in the kitchen woke her with a start. It was almost six. She yawned, then went into the tiny bathroom and ran a brush through her shoulder-length blonde hair, letting it hang loosely around her shoulders. Her blue eyes were bright with anticipation. After shaking the wrinkles out of a light blue knit top with an embroidered yoke and matching leggings, she changed clothes and touched up her make-up. She noticed as she passed by that the large school kitchen was empty, so she headed outside in search of the barbecue pit and her new friends.

The picnic had already begun. Mr. Birch was mindful to introduce her to everyone, and Karen's head was spinning by the time they had made the rounds. She tried frantically to remember names, and who-went-with-who, but since most children weren't sitting with their parents it was a difficult task. She met Mr. Birch's children and was introduced to a group of single women and one single man, most of them new that year. When she finally joined the line there were only a few people ahead of her, and Roxie and Joe behind her for second helpings. The barbecue featured hamburgers on homemade buns, potato salad, pickles, brownies, coffee and punch. Karen's eyes widened at the spread.

"Burger?" a deep male voice asked, and as she looked up to find the face that went with it, her gaze was met with gentle brown eyes and a wide smile. The young man was as dark as she was fair. His unruly brown hair fell into his eyes as he flipped hamburgers, and Karen took an immediate liking to him. "Hi, I'm Rob," he said, extending his hand. "Are you Karen?"

"Yes, hi." She smiled back and shook his hand warmly. "Rob--I've heard a lot about you from Mr. Birch. Did you make all these burgers?"

"Sure did. Lois is sick, so tonight's all on me."

"Oh, my! That's a lot of work--I'll be happy to help you clean up," Karen said sincerely as Rob slid a hamburger onto her plate.

"I'll be happy to let you," he answered, his smile growing wider, "although my manners tell me to turn you down, since it's only your first day and all. Are you sure you don't mind?"

Roxie cleared her throat. "Would anybody mind if *I* had a burger?" she teased, and Rob pretended to frown as he put one on her plate, then flipped several that were ready.

"Not at all," Karen told him, letting Roxie and Joe and a few others pass by her as she lingered to talk to Rob. "I may as well get started. I've got a lot to learn! Besides, I guess we'll be working together."

"That we will." He gave Karen a broad smile, and Karen excused herself to finish dishing up and find a place to sit. She was grateful that Roxie had saved her a seat, and she noticed that Rob took his plate and was sitting by the other single male teacher.

Later, as she and Rob gathered up the leftover food, she complimented him on the special flavor in the burgers. "It really adds something," she told him. "What is it?"

"Thanks. It's my own barbecue sauce," he said sheepishly. "The kids like it. You learn to be creative here. I make my own bacon bits, too, out of ham. Bacon's very expensive, so I fry a few pieces and add the grease to chopped-up ham bits." He seemed eager to share his ideas as they wrapped the various food items and placed them into the large refrigerator.

"What do you do with leftovers?" she asked.

"Use them creatively." He grinned. "Last year we served leftover ham five times before the kids caught on! Let's see," he counted off on his fingers, "scrambled eggs and ham, beans and ham, split pea soup, scalloped potatoes. Bacon bits used the last of it. We try to waste as little food as possible."

Karen laughed. "That *is* creative." Though she had seen the kitchen earlier, she asked Rob to show her around. Eager to dive in headfirst, Karen was full of ideas and plans for the upcoming year. She tentatively shared several of them with Rob.

"I--I was thinking of a birthday party for all twelve months," she explained. "Since there are always those summer birthdays no one gets to celebrate when school is closed, this would be a way of doing that. We could bake twelve cakes, all different flavors and all gaily decorated for that month. For example, September could be a carrot cake, made to look like a little schoolhouse; July could be a flag, and so on. December would be easy." She stopped to catch her breath and gauge Rob's reaction. "Well, what do you think?"

Pleased at her enthusiasm, Rob's brown eyes twinkled. "I think the kids will love it. Did you want us to do all the work ourselves, or let them help?"

"Hmmm. I hadn't really thought that far ahead, but we *could* have the junior girls' dorm make a cake, whatever month they choose; the senior girls could do one, and even the boys, if they want. Maybe a couple of the teachers would like to, too. Then the kitchen could do the rest. I don't suppose it matters. The best part is, then we would have a party to celebrate everyone's birthdays."

"When is yours?" she asked Rob suddenly, aware of his disconcerting gaze upon her.

"Uh--June."

"Ah hah! One of those people I was talking about."

"How about you?"

She blushed, because she was "one of those people" as well. "July," she replied. "I used to feel so left out because my mother never brought cupcakes to school! Then one year she did. In January. For my 'half-birthday', she called it." Her eyes misted at the thought, and a surge of homesickness shot through her.

Rob grinned. "Okay, sounds good. You decide when you want it, and we'll take it from there. In fact, let's go over the year right now, if you're game."

They sat down with pen and paper and Rob went over the scheduled events for the year. Karen's head was spinning. It seemed to her there was cookout, a party, a class outing or a special luncheon every other week!

"Wow" was all she could say.

Rob laughed. "Yeah, exactly. And not everything's on the calendar yet! The rule is, though, if a group expects food from the kitchen, they need to give us *at least* one week's notice. But don't let all this scare you. Remember, one thing at a time, and we've got the maids to help. Where you and I are most needed is to keep everything coordinated. Then, too, there are the special American foods, like foil dinners for campouts, deviled eggs, cheesecake, twice-baked potatoes. Most everything else is second nature to Lucy and Rosalba. And the food's delicious here. Wait until you try *arepas*!"

"A--what?"

"*Arepas*. They're a bit like tacos, but different. A thick batter is made up of cornmeal, then deep fried. Sliced down the middle, you can eat them warm, with fried meat and cheese stuffed inside, or spread with butter and jam."

Karen's mouth was watering. "I think I'm going to gain ten pounds here in the first month alone!"

On impulse, she shared with him her feelings of inadequacy. He assured her that he was there to help and told her several funny anecdotes of the past year. Karen saw what Mr. Birch had meant. Who could *not* get along with Rob?

After Rob left, Karen returned to her apartment alone, surprised that it was after eleven o'clock. Refreshed from her earlier nap, she decided to unpack. Opening her small suitcase first, she removed her toiletries and placed them one by one into the bathroom cabinet. She hung up the few dresses she had brought and placed her socks and undergarments in the dresser drawers. The desk and bookshelves were soon filled with stationery, pens, books, and framed photographs. With those touches, the bedroom was beginning to look like home.

Walking into the living room, she surveyed her surroundings. The place looked as though someone had cleaned it earlier that day. Fresh flowers greeted her from the coffee table, and Karen wondered if that had been done in preparation for her arrival. Suddenly hungry, and realizing it had been five hours since she'd eaten, she opened the refrigerator, wondering as she did so if she could get something to eat from the school's kitchen. To her delight, the fridge contained a carton of milk, several bottled juice drinks, a brick of cheese and a large basket of fruit. "Welcome, Karen!" said a note attached to the basket, with no clue who it was from.

What a lovely gesture, she thought to herself, and pulled a large ripe banana from the top of the pile. *But I wonder why they keep bananas in the refrigerator!* Just then she caught sight of movement out of the corner of her eye. A large black bug scurried across the long kitchen counter. Karen squealed, then laughed at herself. *Welcome to Venezuela,* she thought wryly. She knew that the humid conditions made it easy for cockroaches and other insects to thrive. Rob had mentioned keeping flour and sugar in air-tight bins...but he hadn't mentioned *bug-tight!*

When she finally decided to go to bed, Karen lifted the covers and stretched out between the sheets, letting her thoughts wander back over the day. She had met so many nice people--the teachers and staff families that she would be working with during the year. Karen already liked it here. If people only realized what missionary life was really like, maybe more of them would come--even for a year. Karen smiled, realizing that until now she hadn't even considered herself a missionary. Her idea of a *real* missionary was one who went to the far corners of the earth to tell people about Christ. But wasn't she making it possible for others to do just that, by caring for their children here at the school? Yes, she admitted to herself--*she* was a missionary.

And ready for a new adventure.

CHAPTER TWO

The Adventure Begins

When Karen ventured into the kitchen Monday morning, she was glad that she had until the following weekend to get ready before the students arrived. Since Mr. Birch had given the maids the day off, figuring their life as well as hers would be crazy enough in a week, Karen had planned to fix herself a bowl of cereal in the school kitchen. She wasn't prepared to find Rob already busy at the stove, stirring a colorful concoction that looked like a Spanish omelet.

"Hi," he said, glancing up from the stove. "Hungry?"

"Actually, yes. Figured I'd just have some cereal or something."

"Oh, but you haven't tried my South American Sizzle," he told her, looking wounded. "Do you have a strong stomach?"

Karen laughed. "Well, somewhat. I'm game for anything once."

Pleased, Rob grinned as he dished up two plates. He then walked over to the toaster and popped in four English muffin halves.

"How did you know I wouldn't have already eaten?" she asked him, curious.

"Because I happen to know you don't have any food!" Rob said with a smug look on his face. "Lois told me all she gave you was juice and milk and fruit."

"And cheese," Karen added. "I could have made an eggless omelet or something!"

"Well, I'm glad you didn't," Rob admitted. "I wanted to try this out on you. Here, sit." He motioned to the tall kitchen stool in front of the long counter overlooking the dining hall. "Coffee?"

"Hmm," Karen nodded dreamily as she sat. "Somebody pinch me, I fell asleep last night and woke up in a foreign country where the man waits on the woman!" she teased. "Quite different from *my* country!"

Rob grinned. He seemed to enjoy waiting on her. "Here." He handed her a cup of coffee, then returned with four buttered muffin halves. "Don't mind the fingers, they're semi-clean." As they ate together in amicable silence, Rob glanced over at her anxiously. "Like it?"

The first taste of his creation was delicious, but by the second and third bites Karen's mouth was warming up. "Do you serve water with your meals?" she gasped.

Rob burst out laughing and jumped up to bring her a glass of water. "Spicy, huh?"

"Uh--you could say that. I can see why you call it the 'Sizzle'! It's good though, Rob," she had to admit.

"Really. I just can't take a lot of spicy food. I bet it would be great with a little sour cream."

When they were finished with breakfast, Rob asked, "Well, shall we get down to business?" He rinsed off their plates and put them in the deep sink in a small adjoining room labeled the "Dish Pit".

"Who does the dishes?" Karen asked.

"The kids. Mostly high schoolers, though the younger ones do help. They're not real fast at it, so we try to find other jobs for them. Two high school girls will show up half an hour before breakfasts and suppers, to set up the coffee, set tables, and help wherever needed. Now, let's see...." Rob threw one leg over the stool and sat back down at the counter. "For this final week of summer, the first meal required of the kitchen staff is a school kick-off dinner Saturday night, since most of the out-of-town students will get here on Saturday with their parents. By Sunday almost everyone will have arrived, and by Monday the schedule will be in full swing with three meals a day."

"So that means I have a full five days to get trained, huh?" Karen asked. She didn't know whether to feel scared or relieved.

"Basically. I would suggest that we start by meal planning and making shopping lists, as well as doing a thorough cleaning of the entire kitchen. Now, the maids will help us with that, of course," he explained, taking a sip of his coffee. "But you'll have to tell them what you want done, and I can translate for you if you need me to." He paused. "The maids are great, though. Rosalba understands a little English since she's worked here so long. And Lucy is quick and bright and seems to have a sixth sense about what needs to be done."

"Mr. Birch mentioned that his wife Lois would be here, too."

"Oh, yeah--I hope you don't mind, but I told Lois we'd call her if we need her help," Rob admitted. "She's still not feeling very well, and she has her hands full with her regular responsibilities besides. I think she was relieved when I told her we probably wouldn't need her."

Karen nodded her assent. They each poured themselves a second cup of coffee and sat perched on the tall stools.

"Just between you and me, I think she's pregnant," Rob said mysteriously.

"Really?"

"Yup. I'm the oldest of six kids, so I know all the symptoms. And besides, Paul and Lois want at least four children and only have two so far."

Karen smiled. "No announcements yet, though."

Rob shook his head. "No, and please don't say anything. Call it a hunch on my part. But with that in mind, I really didn't feel we could ask for her help.

Besides, I think you and I will do fine." He gave Karen a broad smile that caused Karen to catch her breath. Somehow, she, too, felt they would do just *fine*. With Rob's self-assurance and calm, easy manner, what could go wrong?

"Also, I can go over the budget with you," Rob continued. "It won't make a bit of sense at this point, though, since their monetary system is so different from ours and you probably have no idea what things cost. Actually--" he tore a sheet of paper from his notebook. "The school board wants to try something new this year. Some of the high school guys have complained that they don't get enough meat. Consequently, the parents call to find out if we're feeding them enough!

"The problem is," he went on, "high school guys eat a lot, and we can't always give them three and four burgers. We tell them to eat other stuff as well, which doesn't make them too happy. But to appease the parents, and make sure the money is being spent the way it ought to be, the school board devised a plan."

Karen found herself lost in his words. Not just his words, but his voice and the anticipation of the year ahead were making her a little dizzy. Yes, it was a big job, but she was beginning to feel up to the challenge. Especially with Rob at her side.

"Make sense?" he was asking.

She nodded eagerly.

"So the 'A' meals are meals where the main dish is meat, such as pork chops, steak, barbecued chicken, et cetera. 'B' meals consist of things like tacos--which, incidentally, is their favorite--also sweet and sour pork, lasagna, spaghetti. 'C' meals are meals with less meat, like hot dogs, submarine sandwiches, tomato soup and toasted cheese sandwiches. We have to serve so many of each type of meal every week."

"Do I have to figure out which meal is what type?" Karen asked.

"Those are pretty well set," he told her. "And we always have an 'A' meal for Sunday dinner, and Saturday lunch is always leftovers! Anything left after Saturday lunch gets thrown out."

"Sounds fine with me."

By the end of the day Karen was tired but happy. She was ready with a list of tasks when the maids returned the next day. The meal plans for the first two weeks were complete, Rob had his shopping list in hand, and Karen knew where each basic item in the kitchen was located.

And she had already made one friend.

The week went quickly by, as Karen got acquainted with Lucy and Rosalba and learned the Spanish words for most of the baking ingredients. Together they cleaned and organized, labeled and restocked. By Thursday the kitchen was clean and in order, and the maids had baked bread ahead and placed it in the freezer. Friday was reserved for preparing the kick-off dinner for Saturday night.

As she and Rob had talked about the kick-off dinner, Karen voiced her concerns. "I'm torn between serving pork chops and *arroz con pollo*," she confided. "Roxie said that last year they served barbecued chicken, but somehow that just doesn't seem special enough. And it's kind of messy. Besides, I don't want to have the same thing two years in a row."

Rob was thoughtful as he chewed his pencil. "Hmm. True."

Karen brightened as an idea formed in her mind. "Rob, have you ever served Chicken Cordon Bleu?"

Rob's eyes widened. "Actually, no, and that's one of my personal favorites. Have you made it before?"

"No, but I'm sure I could find a good recipe. We could serve it with rice pilaf, mixed vegetables, some kind of fruit salad, and maybe even Caesar salad!"

Rob let out a hoot. "Lady, you *do* have taste. But what about our budget?"

"Our budget?" The smile disappeared from Karen's face. "Would that meal be expensive?"

"Actually, the most expensive items besides the Swiss cheese would be the romaine lettuce and parmesan cheese for Caesar salad. But I'd sure like to give it a try. Just remember, if we're over-budget the very first meal, you may have to make up for it the rest of the week!" he said with a twinkle in his eye.

"It would be worth it," Karen said firmly, determined to make her idea work.

The meal preparation went off without a hitch. Rob had found the necessary food items at reasonable prices, and a cookbook of Roxie's contained the perfect recipe for the chicken. By late Friday children began to arrive for classes, and the compound of connected buildings became a hubbub of activity. Karen spent most of Saturday in the kitchen, assisting the maids in preparing the special food and setting the tables with matching tablecloths. Lucy shaped the homemade rolls into crescent shapes while Karen scooped butterballs and dished up bowls of jam. French silk pies sat cooling on the counter.

Karen stood back with a contented look and surveyed the situation. For being the first meal she was in charge of, she was feeling quite pleased with how things were turning out. Now all that remained was for her to change clothes and prepare *herself* for the evening. Rob had disappeared moments earlier, promising to return before the first parent arrived.

Karen's feet were already tired, and she was looking forward to a long, relaxing shower. But first, she noticed that her dirty laundry, which was piled up in a cardboard box in a corner, was overflowing. Quickly she walked down the hall to the laundry room and loaded two washers full, then went back to her room and jumped in the shower.

As the spray pelted off of her skin and hair, she reveled in it, letting the warmth of the water invigorate her. After lathering her hair and body, she was just about to rinse off when the spray suddenly stopped coming out of the nozzle.

Karen screamed.

Quickly turning the handles, she found that no matter what she did no water would come. Wondering if Venezuela had plumbers, she grabbed the bath towel and made her way into her little kitchen, grateful that the curtains were closed. When no water would come from the kitchen faucet either, she panicked. There was no way she could go to a banquet with shampoo in her hair!

Roxie. Roxie had mentioned keeping bottled water for the girls to drink. She quickly called Roxie, but no one answered. Then she remembered Roxie and Joe had driven to the airport to pick up a carload of arriving students.

Wracking her brain, Karen considered the teakettle. Remembering she had fixed herself a cup of tea the other evening, she knew the kettle should still be almost full. Grabbing the kettle by the handle, she ran back into the shower, stripped off the towel, and slowly poured the entire contents over her head. But the teakettle had only been halfway full, and she could still feel sticky remains of soap in her blonde strands. Wondering what effect milk would have on her hair, she quickly decided against it and began to blow-dry the wet strands.

Well, at least there's still electricity, she thought ruefully as she ran the hot air back and forth over her head. Oh, no! If there was no water here, there would be no water in the large kitchen, either! And the tables had already been beautifully decorated with the school's standard glass dishes. A tear began to trickle out of one eye and was soon joined by another.

Stay calm, Karen, keep your head. Maybe Rob would know what to do.

Just then she heard a knock at the door. Hoping it was Roxie, she threw on a robe and ran frantically through the adjoining room to open the front door.

"Rob!"

"Uh--hi! I guess you're not ready yet."

"Not exactly!" she said sarcastically. "The shower went off before I could rinse my hair! And what will we do about the dishes?" Chagrined, she began to close the door. "I can't talk now. I'll meet you in the kitchen as soon as I'm dressed."

Karen shut the door in his face and ran back to the bedroom. Then, realizing she had been rude, she ran back and opened the door just as Rob was turning away.

"Rob! I'm sorry!"

He grinned, looking her up and down in amusement. "That's okay. I just wanted to ask you if you want to switch to paper plates."

"But the table's already set! And the maids left an hour ago!"

Rob glanced at his watch. "I know. It'll be tight, but I can start now if you want. The thing is, the water shutoff usually only lasts an hour or two. Just until the tank can get filled up again. We can stick to glass if you want. The catch is, if the water doesn't come on before the end of the evening, we'll have a pretty sticky mess to clean up. Dishes are on us this first meal or two, until we can get a schedule lined up for the students."

Karen did some quick thinking. "Let's stick to glass. If I have to, I'll go in the dish pit at two in the morning and wash dishes! I just want everything to be perfect for the banquet!"

"Perfect? In Venezuela?" Rob said jokingly. "Okay. That's fine with me. But don't call me at two a.m. Three, maybe." He grinned. "I'll let you get dressed now. See you in a bit." He turned and walked nonchalantly down the hall.

Karen was fuming. How could the man be so calm? Apparently, the lack of water had not ruined *his* shower or *his* hair. He'd had a good ten-minute start on her and had much less hair to contend with. What was more, *he* hadn't put two loads of laundry in to wash!

Oh well. It was probably best that one of them could stay calm; it might as well be Rob. Now to concentrate on her hair.

When Karen reappeared in the large kitchen half an hour later, she hoped that the few students and parents lingering around were paying more attention to her brightly-colored orchid print dress than to her hairdo. Usually well-behaved in a simple straight style, her hair felt dry to the touch and seemed to be sticking out on all sides. She felt like crying but knew that would be overly vain. What mattered now was how the dinner turned out. And, she admitted, making a good impression on the parents.

Rob glanced up as she entered and suppressed a grin. "Hi," he said, seemingly oblivious to her appearance. Then he said mischievously, "Aw shucks, you changed clothes. I kind of liked that red terrycloth thing you were wearing."

Karen didn't know whether to laugh or be angry. She stared at him for a moment, and Rob's face broke into a wide smile. At that, she started to cry.

"Uh--sorry, Karen, I was just teasing. You look fine, really. Uh--I like your dress."

She sniffed. "Thanks. I'll be okay in a minute--just first-meal jitters. Any water yet?"

"Not yet. I left the dish pit faucet on, so we'll know the minute it comes on. Unfortunately, we can't make coffee until it does. Good thing the punch is already mixed up."

Karen sighed and glanced at the large clock on the kitchen wall. Half an hour until dinner. More students and parents were beginning to file through the door, high school boys coming early out of hunger and junior girls anxious to take their parents upstairs to see their rooms.

"Well," Karen said, forcing a smile from behind her tears. "Here goes. D-day."

Rob grinned at her. "That's the spirit."

Just then the water faucet began to sputter. Karen let out a shriek. There would be coffee with dessert after all.

CHAPTER THREE

A Trip to the City

K aren had been in Venezuela for less than a month when Rob asked her to accompany him to San Cristobal, a larger city about an hour away. She heard a rap at her door one Sunday evening and called out, "Just a minute." Expecting Roxie, seeing Rob standing there was a pleasant surprise. He shifted his weight uneasily from one foot to the other, his stalky frame filling the doorway.

He seemed nervous. "Uh, Karen, I was wondering. Um--would you want to go to San Cristobal with me tomorrow, since it's your day off? I need to run a couple of errands. There's a basket place I thought you might like."

"Oh! I *would*!" Karen agreed. "I'd like to get a big basket for my laundry."

He smiled and let out his breath. "Okay, we'll take my jeep. I'll come by tomorrow morning around ten."

"But--don't you have a computer class?" Karen asked.

"Not on Mondays." He grinned. "See you tomorrow."

Karen smiled to herself after closing the door. Was this the same self-assured Rob that she worked with side by side every day? Why would he be nervous about asking her to join him? Well never mind, she was glad that he had.

The following morning Karen carefully selected what to wear on her first trip to the city. By nine-thirty it was already stifling hot. Remembering Mr. Birch's caution on shorts, she chose a cotton knit shirt with matching blue flowered skirt. Friends always told her that blue was her best color. The skirt was long enough that she could go bare-legged and wear sandals and be plenty cool. She gave herself a glance of approval in the mirror, slipped in tiny flower earrings, and walked into the living room.

She straightened up her apartment, putting away the book she had been reading the night before and wiping the counter from where she had sliced bread that morning. Then she walked across the hall to the kitchen to make sure her substitute had meal plans under control.

"It'll be fine," Barb assured her. "It isn't like I haven't done this before, you know."

Karen laughed. The woman had been head cook herself one year and now taught piano lessons and raised her three children. In spite of the woman's experience, Karen couldn't help feel a little guilty at leaving the work behind for someone else. But the guilt was soon overcome by the excitement at the prospect of spending her entire day off with Rob. Just getting away from Rubio for a day would have pleased her, but Rob.... Karen sighed. She would need to keep her feelings in check. After all, she was only here for a year, and Rob had already been here one year and said he planned on many more. He was, as she considered him, a "lifer."

When Rob arrived, she was just gathering up her shoulder bag and a light sweater in case it rained. Upon opening the door, she noted with pleasure the gleam in Rob's eye as he greeted her. His eyes silently approved of what she was wearing, and she smiled to herself. Her friends were right. Blue *was* her best color.

"Ready?" he asked.

"You bet." She locked the door behind her, called a quick goodbye to Barb as they passed the kitchen, and walked outside. Rob opened the door for her to get inside, ignoring a wolf whistle coming from somewhere nearby.

As the jeep rambled over the dusty roads and they headed out of town, Karen noticed how naturally Rob seemed to fit into the culture. He knew the road by heart, slowed down at all the uneven landscapes, swerved at the children walking on the road, honked at the dogs about to cross the path in front of the jeep. It didn't seem to bother him that a landslide had half-covered their lane at one point or that they were stuck behind a slow truck for three miles before they could pass.

"What does that mean?" she asked, noting the words "*CARGA LARGA*" on the large truck ahead.

"Long cargo," Rob explained. He kept talking as they drove along, his striped blue and white knit shirt open at the throat. Karen couldn't help noticing how tan and muscular he was. She suddenly gasped as a car sped past them on a mountain curve, with barely enough room to pull back over. Rob's brown eyes twinkled as he glanced over at Karen clutching the door handle.

"Think you wanna drive?" he asked.

"No, thanks! It's hard enough to be a passenger."

He smiled. "You'll get used to it."

"That's what everyone says. I'll probably just be getting used to it by the time I leave!"

Rob was silent for a moment, then murmured, "Just here for a year, huh?"

"Hmm hmm."

"Why did you come?" he asked, genuinely interested.

Karen didn't hesitate in her answer. "I knew this was where God wanted me. I supported the school financially for a couple of years, through our church. So, when the mission representative came to my church in Seattle 'recruiting', I suddenly realized that was what the Lord wanted." She shook her head. "Though I still can't believe He brought me here as 'head cook'! But, as the representative explained, it's mostly meal planning, supervising, making breakfasts and serving Sunday meals. I'm organized, and I felt I could do a good job."

He glanced sideways at her. "Are you saying you don't cook?"

She laughed. "No, I really don't! I mean, I get by okay. It's just not what you'd call a 'great love.' Mostly I've been too busy in my 'other life' at the law firm to spend a lot of time in the kitchen. Sometimes I would have to work ten-hour days and then just grab a burger on the way home. If it weren't for Lucy and Rosalba being here, the kids would probably starve! And YOU, of course," she added sheepishly.

He grinned. "My mom was that way. Six kids later and she *still* says she doesn't cook!" They both laughed. "Do you have sisters and brothers, Karen?"

"No, I'm an only child."

"Wasn't that lonely, growing up with no sisters or brothers?"

Karen shook her head. "No, not at all. The doctor didn't think Mom could have any children, so my parents have always made me feel like I was a special blessing. We did many things together as a family. Probably more than a lot of families. And I could always take a friend along if I wanted. My parents are really super."

"Mine, too," Rob admitted. "And still together after thirty years! Though I think they're a minority these days!"

For the next twenty minutes they chatted about Rob growing up on a farm in Colorado, then the conversation turned to the kitchen. They both shared ideas for snacks and upcoming menus.

"Let's check on oranges today, too," Karen suggested. "I'd love some fresh juice for the week."

"Good idea."

The basket place was more than Karen had expected. White wicker, green grass baskets, and even flat woven baskets hung from the walls and ceiling of the little shop. The prices confused her, but after Rob explained them, she selected a large basket with a hinged lid for her dirty laundry and a small wicker shelf for her bedroom wall. Fortunately, Mr. Birch had traded her American money for local currency, and she knew she had enough on hand to last her the rest of the month.

They stopped for lunch at a stand on the street. "These burgers are unbeatable," Rob said. "You've got to try one. I wish they had these in the States." The six-inch hamburger buns were filled with cooked burger, a slice of cheese, tiny French-fried potatoes, sauce, ham, a fried egg, and a slice of fresh avocado. Karen agreed they were delicious and tried not to consider how much fat they contained. It wasn't until after consuming the entire sandwich that Rob admitted, "People will warn you about eating food sold on the street. But I've never had any problem."

"What do you mean?" Karen asked, wide-eyed.

"Parasites. But don't worry--I've been here over a year and haven't been sick once. The most important thing is not to drink the water unless it's been filtered or boiled."

Karen tried not to let the comment bother her. If Rob said it was okay, it must be okay. She certainly did not want to get sick her first month here!

Rob seemed pleased at Karen's wonderment as he showed her around the city. He pointed out a large supermarket and said, "That one's similar to a grocery store in the States--nice long, clean aisles, variety... not like the little stores in Rubio. You can find practically anything there. Of course, you pay a pretty price for it, too."

He pointed out the dress shops, the pharmacies, the paper supply stores. "No Walmart here," he explained. "It's pretty much one store per item." He showed her the *panaderia* where, he boasted, they had wonderful bread and pastries. "I'll take you there sometime," he promised. "And if Roxie ever brings you, I'm sure she'll show you all the dress shops and shoe stores!"

"I hope so!" Karen admitted.

They stopped in at the large post office to check for mail. "Why doesn't the mail come to Rubio?" Karen asked.

"It does, if you want to wait another couple of days," Rob explained. "There *is* a post office in Rubio, but most of the time someone's coming to the city anyway, so it's more convenient for us this way. We don't even give out the Rubio address anymore."

As the day wore on, Karen was indeed beginning to appreciate the culture and the scenery of this lovely South American country. Some of the flowers were the most unusual she had ever seen. Poinsettias were in full bloom. Trees were a deep, lush green from all the rain. Karen's favorite shrub very much resembled a rosebush, covered with what looked like tiny rosebuds. She had been a nature lover in the States, but the scenery here was incomparable.

They arrived back at the school just in time for supper. For the last few weeks Karen had eaten in her apartment on her day off, preferring the solitude after a busy week. But after Rob helped her carry the baskets to her room, they went through the meal line together, then Karen sat down across from Joe and Roxie and their girls. Rob carried his plate across the room to sit with some high school boys. *That's funny*, Karen mused, then caught herself. After all, it wasn't like they were a couple. She quickly recovered and filled Roxie in on the events of the day. Before leaving the dining hall, she glanced over at Rob. He caught her eye and winked.

CHAPTER FOUR

Starting a Bible Club

Karen continued to set the thick glass coffee cups and saucers on a platter, then refilled the sugar container and added fresh milk to the small pitcher. Since the high schoolers were all away at a spiritual emphasis retreat for three days, Karen was doing the jobs the girls normally did. The repetitive tasks set her to thinking.

"Rob," she began, "why do we have someone do this every single morning?"

"What do you mean? So, we can have our coffee, of course!"

"No, silly--I mean, why not make a permanent counter of some sort just outside the kitchen where the coffeepot is kept and the coffee cups are put away each day, rather than spending our time restocking?"

Rob's eyes gleamed with understanding. "You mean, a permanent coffee bar. With cupboards and shelves. Karen, that's a great idea. To tell you the truth, I don't know why no one thought of it before. I don't know why I didn't think of it myself! That would eliminate a big part of the high school girls' morning routine."

"Exactly. Do you suppose the shop teacher would build us a cabinet?"

"We won't know until we ask. Let's hit him up after *he's* had his first cup!" Rob grinned.

When Doug and his wife Cindy entered the dining hall and Karen flashed them a friendly smile, Doug sauntered over to the counter as usual. "Morning," he said, his quick nod acknowledging them both.

"Morning," Rob said as he scooped large portions of fluffy scrambled eggs into bowls to be carried to the tables. He watched out of the corner of his eye as Doug added two teaspoonfuls of sugar, then a generous portion of milk to the steaming coffee. "Got a minute?" Rob handed the bowls of food to Roxie to take to the tables, then scooped portions into the two remaining bowls.

Doug took his first sip of coffee and smiled. "Shoot."

Karen continued arranging the warm muffins on platters as she watched from the corner of her eye. The rest of the group was trickling in, and breakfast would begin in a few minutes. Doug continued to sip his coffee while Rob animatedly explained about the desired project. She saw Doug's face take on an expression of concentration, then he nodded. The next thing she knew, Rob was motioning her over.

"Karen, exactly what proportions would we want?"

"I don't know, but we could sure draw something up after you and I talk about it some more. Could we give the plans to you later today, Doug?"

"Sure. I'm not going anywhere. I've got a roof to patch!" he said, grinning. Besides being the senior boys' dorm parents, Cindy and Doug, like everyone else on the staff, were kept busy in many other ways. Doug was the school's shop teacher, and when something needed fixing, he was the first one to be asked. He was an expert carpenter, so the more specialized jobs needed his expertise.

"That's a good idea," Doug said in his low Canadian drawl as he walked away and grinned at the two of them. "Shouldn't be difficult to construct."

Karen met Rob's eye and grinned at him.

To Karen's delight, within the week Doug had begun work on the coffee bar. He consulted her often with questions about proportions, and suggested things Karen had not thought of. By the time it was finished, it was not only serviceable but very attractive. Constructed of sturdy plywood, the large flat countertop had plenty of area for the coffeepot, a plain hot water dispenser, a sugar bowl, and a cream pitcher. Off to one side there were containers with hot chocolate packets and teabags. A cupboard for extra cups was in the spacious cabinet underneath.

On the morning the coffee bar officially opened, the high school servers were thrilled. "What a great idea, Aunt Karen," they told her. Karen was still getting used to being everyone's "aunt" but found herself warming to the affectionate title.

"Don't worry, I'll still find plenty of work for you in the mornings!" she warned the girls.

They only laughed. "I'm sure you will."

Roxie walked in just then. "Karen, I'd like to talk to you after breakfast if you've got a minute. I'll come by after the girls leave for school, okay?"

"Sure."

Karen was just finishing her own breakfast when Roxie reappeared forty minutes later. Roxie poured herself a cup of coffee and sat down across from her.

"I've got something I want you to consider, Karen. Would you be interested in helping me with a Bible club for a group of children up in the hills?"

"What? *Me*?" Karen faltered. "I can't even speak much Spanish!"

Roxie laughed. "That's okay, you don't really need to. And besides, it might be a nice change from the kitchen. Several of us have been going up in the hills weekly to tell stories, sing, and play games with about fifteen children. Their parents are originally from Columbia and are very poor. They really look forward to our weekly visit. We also serve refreshments-- cookies and juice, or milk when we can afford it."

Karen thought it over. "I suppose I wouldn't need Spanish to help with games or serve refreshments. When is the next meeting?"

"On Saturday. I know that's a busy time for you, since the maids leave early that day, but Rob already said--"

"Aha! A conspiracy," Karen's voice accused, but her eyes twinkled at the thought.

"No--" stammered Roxie as she shook her layered brown curls from side to side. "I happened to be talking to him the other day, and he said that since lunch is usually leftovers anyway, he wouldn't mind doing it alone. As long as you're back in time to do the picnic with him."

Karen was thoughtful. "What about having the Bible club during the week?"

"We could try that. The kids are in school during the week, though, and Saturday is pretty well established with them."

"Oh, of course. What made you think of me, anyway?"

"Well," said Roxie, "I know you like kids, and Kelly has to quit club because of a heavy teaching load. She's already coaching the girls' soccer team and acting as one of the sponsors of the sophomore class--besides teaching all of the English classes."

"Wow. People here really stretch themselves thin, don't they?" Karen mused.

"We have to, with so few of us to do so many jobs. But Karen, the first day I went to the Bible club, I was hooked. The children are so full of love and so much fun. It's a real bright spot in their week. And mine. I just know you'd love it. And they would love you. Will you think it over?"

Karen smiled. "I just did. I'm in!"

The next Bible club was on Saturday, and true to his word, Rob agreed to serve lunch alone. The kitchen even had extra cake from a high school social that he suggested the group take for the snack. "We don't always have extra," he explained. "And even though it's all for the mission, the school is on a separate budget, so we can't just give things away. But when we have leftover food like this, feel free to use it. It would probably go to waste otherwise. And anyway," his eyes twinkled, "it isn't like we can serve it in scrambled eggs all week!"

Karen smiled. "Who pays for the Bible club food?" she asked.

"Probably the women. Sometimes church groups send money for things like that. Last year a youth group sent a hundred dollars, and they bought shoes for that whole group of kids. The families are so poor they usually go barefoot. That's okay in the summertime, in fact a lot of kids do, but during rainy season it's awful."

Karen sobered. She had never met anyone that poor. Even the panhandlers in Seattle wore shoes. Momentarily subdued, she made no comment as Rob helped her put the cake into plastic containers. She grabbed a package of paper napkins, thanked him, and left. "See you around three-thirty," she called out.

"Remember, I'm doing deviled eggs for the picnic tonight. Have the maids boil about six dozen, okay?"

He nodded. "Have fun."

She jumped into Roxie's waiting car where Kelly, one of the school's other single women, sat in the back. They drove up steep winding roads and Karen slowly began to take in the poverty around her. The houses here were unlike any she had seen in the lower part of Rubio. The higher up they drove, the worse the living conditions became. Most houses had no glass over the windows, only small square openings in the walls. Wet clothes hung from lines stretched from one end of the yard to the other. Women with dirty aprons and no shoes washed clothes in tubs outside. A man, apparently drunk, his bottle clutched in one hand, was lying at the side of the road mumbling, and Roxie swerved to avoid him. Karen gasped.

Roxie had already warned Karen not to bring any money with her, as any American was easy prey, especially women. It wasn't just that people would steal money--they would ask for it, and it was simpler to honestly say, "*no tengo*" than to refuse them. There was no end to those who asked, Roxie told her. She explained that at times she did give, but it was usually in the form of food, not money. Too many of the men would have simply spent money on liquor and left their families with nothing to eat.

When they arrived at the compound of homes where the Bible club was held, the stench hit Karen even before getting out of the car. She braced herself and tried to breathe in some of the cologne she had dabbed on her wrist earlier. The children noisily swarmed around the truck with excited exclamations. Karen was surprised to find that she understood several of their words. A child's Spanish was closer to that of her own, not like the street vendors whose many dialects were spoken too quickly for her to grasp.

"*Hola! Hola!*" she called, and they came over to where she stood. Roxie introduced her to the children while they chattered and smiled. Their dirty little faces were bright with smiles as they thronged the three women.

Karen immediately noticed one little boy who made loud shrieks rather than talking. He was small-boned, with cute impish features, and reminded her of a little monkey. She shot Roxie a puzzled glance. Roxie explained that the boy was deaf and unable to speak, and she directed the boy's attention to Karen. He smiled shyly at Karen and made noises from his throat.

"His name is Pedro," said Roxie. "And this is Carmelina, his mother." She indicated a woman who stood shyly in the background wiping her dirty hands on an already filthy apron. The woman smiled and nodded, and Karen smiled back. Karen's own bright cotton pants were a sharp contrast to the woman's drab housedress. Karen wondered briefly if the church groups ever sent used clothing.

"Let's do games first," suggested Roxie, and Karen immediately turned her attention back to the children. Kelly led the children in "Duck, Duck, Goose", then played several other games in quick succession, and the kids chattered delightedly.

"'Button, button' is fun too," Kelly told Karen. "Even the simplest things work great here. These kids don't have video games and computers and every new toy to play with like kids in the States."

With games over, the children gathered into a circle without being told. Roxie captivated their attention with a Bible story told in Spanish illustrated with large, colorful pictures. The young audience seemed enthralled and raised their hands to answer Roxie's questions. Karen didn't understand what they were saying, but she saw their eyes widen when Roxie must have announced it was time for cake. Seeing the children's delight at the cake and milk, Karen told herself she wanted to do refreshments every week. She would take some of her own time and money and prepare something special. And healthy, like cheese and crackers or even peanut butter and jelly sandwiches. Maybe she could have Rob pick her up a stalk of bananas.

It was easy to see that the children were not properly nourished. Roxie had said their parents raised garlic and sold it for a living, but that barely made enough money to provide the stark necessities. At times even flour and potatoes were a rarity. The large family, consisting of the grandparents, eight adult children and their spouses, and twenty-one grandchildren, lived in close proximity to each other, with an outhouse being the only bathroom. Their living conditions made Karen shudder, each home being a one-room cement block, in most cases the only opening being the doorway. Karen was just glad she would be able to brighten their day for an hour or two each week.

When it was time to leave, the children waved goodbye, then crowded around the car as it pulled away. The little hands continued to wave until the car had turned a corner and was out of sight.

Karen was quiet on the drive home, and Roxie flashed her an understanding smile. "You're already hooked, aren't you?" she asked quietly.

Karen nodded, and a tear slid down her cheek. Then, brightening, she asked, "What about 'Pin the Tail on the Donkey'? Have they ever played that? And what about having the school puppet team come out some Saturday and doing a special show just for them?"

Roxie grinned, recognizing in Karen her own enthusiasm the first time she had come. The three women shared ideas all the way back to the dorm, then sat out front talking until Karen remembered her deviled eggs. "I gotta go!" she told Roxie, hurrying into the kitchen. For once, Rob was nowhere to be found, but Karen didn't mind. She pulled the pan of eggs from the refrigerator anticipating peeling each one and noted gratefully that the maids had already peeled the six dozen hardboiled eggs. She worked in silence as she cut each egg in half and spooned out the yolk. Then she mashed the yolks in a bowl and added salad dressing, mustard, and salt, and a tiny dab of horseradish. Just after she had spooned the mixture back into the egg halves, Rob reappeared. After a quick greeting, Karen sprinkled paprika on top, then sprang into action as she and Rob loaded food onto trays for the picnic.

"How did club go?" Rob asked her.

"Oh, good, real good," she replied. "I've offered to bring snack every week. Those poor kids--" Her voice trailed off along with her thoughts. As they worked side by side, Karen knew she was quieter than usual, but Rob made no comment.

Karen was still quiet as she and Rob cleared the food and put it away later that evening. They worked amicably together, but Karen found that she was weary. For some reason it seemed like a very long day.

"By the way, thanks for having the maids peel the eggs," Karen told Rob. "They must have really had to hustle, because I know they like to leave early on Saturday, and when I got back, they were already gone."

Rob only smiled mysteriously and said good night. As Karen prepared for bed, she couldn't help remembering that smile. Had he peeled the eggs himself? Grinning, she decided to ask Rosalba on Monday, without Rob knowing.

Thinking back over the day, she couldn't help picturing in her mind the children's faces. And Pedro's among them. Since he was deaf, he couldn't go to school with the others. There didn't seem to be a place for him without the money to go along with it. His life would be bleak enough without being deaf as well. What kind of a future would he face?

Karen was determined to find a way to help him.

In bed she tossed and turned. Gradually she had learned to sleep through the night noises so common here--the trucks driving by, the dogs barking, the clang, clang of the metal fences. That night, she heard them all. Finally, she drifted off to a restless sleep.

CHAPTER FIVE

News from Home

M ail," Rob called out, having just returned from a buying trip. He tossed a letter onto the counter, and Karen's heart skipped a beat.

She had not heard from Jeff since she'd arrived five weeks ago. Though he had not promised to wait for her, in her heart she still carried a small flicker of hope that he would change his mind. Perhaps, on missing her, he would decide to wait after all.

Karen's mood plummeted quickly when she noted that the writing was in her mother's familiar longhand. Of course, it was her mom. Jeff, if he wrote at all, would have texted or emailed. Grateful to hear news of home, though, she quickly laid aside the batter she was stirring and tore open the flap.

Her mother's words were cheery, as always, telling of local rainy weather and events of the church and the city. Mrs. Houck had given birth to her third baby, two weeks overdue, and old Mr. Miller across the street had died. Karen's cat was doing fine. Her parents were taking a short vacation to Idaho soon to visit relatives.

Then gently, at the very end of the letter, her mother had written:

> Karen, I may as well tell you, Jeff has started dating Melinda from church. She seems quite taken with him. Don't feel too bad--his lack of understanding about your commitment to God's will clearly says he wasn't the man for you. Love always, Mom.

Karen broke into tears and hurried across the hall to the privacy of her apartment. *The louse,* she thought angrily. *We were practically engaged, and he can't even wait two months! And Melinda, that--that--airhead!* She threw herself onto the bed and cried, until she heard a soft knock at the living room door. Wiping her eyes, she walked to the door and opened it.

Rob stood there, uncertain. "I--uh--just wondered what to do with the green beans," he stammered. "Do you want Rosalba and Lucy to prepare them for cooking or should they just go in the fridge until tomorrow?" He was studying her face intently as he spoke.

"I don't care," she said, sniffing, then realized she was being rude. "I'm--I'm sorry, Rob. The maids are expecting them. They're going to get them ready today, and we'll put them on to cook tomorrow. Please thank Señor Mantilla for me."

Rob waited.

"Was there something else?"

"Yeah--are you *okay*? Was there--bad news from home?"

The tears began to flow again, and she bit her lip. "Yes--I mean, no--not really."

"Not really okay?"

"That too." She sniffed. Rob looked confused, and she motioned him into the room and closed the door behind him.

"I--it's just that--a friend of mine--at least, he *was* a friend--a boyfriend, actually--well, he started going out with someone else."

"Oh. Were you--close?"

"We were practically engaged before I came, but--he didn't understand about my 'sudden fancy to come to Venezuela.'"

Why was she telling him all this? she suddenly wondered. But, since most of the women were older, and married, Rob *was* the closest thing she had for a friend here. Besides Roxie.

Rob nodded solemnly. "I see. Some people don't understand the call to the mission field. Most Christians do, but not all."

Karen sniffed. "Everyone else did. Christians, I mean. The people at my office didn't understand, but at least they were supportive, for the most part. They want me back in a year, but they seemed excited for me to go."

Rob was thoughtful. "That's right, you're only here for a year, huh?"

"Hmm hmm." She almost broke into a smile. "You keep asking me that."

"I know, but it's too bad. You're pretty good at running that kitchen."

She blushed. "Thanks, but--I'm also good at drafting contracts and transcribing documents, which is what I do in my 'other life'. That's what I hope to be back doing by next summer."

His brown eyes faded with disappointment. "Yeah. Well, anyway--I'm sorry about your friend."

"Thanks."

"And don't forget--you promised to go to the market with me in San Cristobal tomorrow."

"Oh--yeah. Uh--we can leave right after breakfast."

"Okay, but don't eat--I want to take you to that bread place with the unbeatable pastries--they have *café con leche*, too. Your favorite." He gave her a warm smile.

Karen half-smiled and sniffed again. She had enjoyed espresso in the States, but nothing could top this traditional "coffee with milk" the South American countries were so well known for--a little very strong coffee, a lot of hot milk, with sugar to make it sweet. "Sounds too good to pass up," she responded, in a vain attempt to be cheerful.

Rob left, then, and she let out a long sigh. It *was* too bad she would only be here a year--or too bad that Rob was committed for longer. But she hadn't stayed in Washington state for a man, and she certainly wasn't about to stay in South America for one. For that reason, Karen intended to keep their friendship on a purely platonic level. She didn't need heartbreak in a foreign country, too!

The next morning, she and Rob fixed French toast, scrambled eggs, fresh cantaloupe, coffee, and milk. After all of the students and teachers had vacated the dining hall and the leftovers were put away, the maids arrived. With Rob's help translating, Karen went over the list of food preparation for the day.

"Are you sure they can handle lunch alone?" Karen asked.

"No problem," Rob assured her. "They did it all the time last year." He again explained to the maids that they were going to the city for the day but would be back in time to finish preparing supper.

"Let's go," he said, and they headed for his jeep.

The drive was peaceful, despite the usual potholes and cars passing with very little room to spare. Karen was getting used to it by now, and she felt confident of Rob's driving ability. At least enough to stop clutching the door handle.

She let out a deep sigh without realizing it.

"What?" Rob asked.

She giggled. "It's just good to get away. Sometimes at the school I feel kind of... cooped up."

"I know what you mean," Rob agreed. "I think that's why I like to go to the market. There really isn't much to do in Rubio. Besides, you and I are both pretty *married* to that kitchen!"

"To be sure." Karen smiled to herself. It was good to have a friend here, too. Other than Rob there was only Roxie to whom she felt close. All of the staff were nice to her and treated her like family, but they were so busy. The teachers had families of their own, and the other single women had their roommates as friends-- Kelly with Jennifer, Amanda with Cathy.

He glanced sideways at her. "What are you smiling about?"

She laughed. "I don't know. I guess I'm just-- happy. Starting to feel a tiny bit like I belong."

"You better believe it," he said firmly, holding his gaze on her for a moment. "Do you know that you were an answer to prayer?"

She blushed. "Yes, that's what Mr. Birch told me. But--I mean, like I belong. Not homesick or anything. Just glad to be here." Then, almost to herself she added, "Besides, my ties with home are even more broken now than before...."

Rob did not respond, and they drove in silence for a while. They entered the busy part of town and Rob searched for a parking place. After treating her to his favorite pastries and *café con leche*, they left the *panaderia* and headed for several warehouses to buy canned goods. The vendors seemed especially curious about Karen, and not a bit ashamed of watching her every move.

"Why are they staring at me?" she finally asked Rob when they were alone in the jeep.

Rob's dark eyes twinkled as he responded to her question. "You're white, you're blonde, and you're pretty," he teased. "Need I say more?"

Karen laughed, but his comment flustered her. Did *he* think she was pretty? She was beginning to understand why it was important to dress modestly and behave appropriately in a foreign country. What she did and how she carried herself reflected not only on herself, but on the school, her country, and the God she represented. Noting that the Venezuelan women always dressed up when going to town, Karen had again worn a skirt and blouse. Since the day was a bit cool, she had chosen a denim skirt with a long-sleeved turtleneck sweater. It seemed silly to be so dressy while riding in a jeep in the middle of the afternoon, but Karen was beginning to appreciate the South American customs. And she would rather be noticed for being "white, blonde, and pretty" than for being sloppy or having on too short of a skirt.

As she and Rob stood talking to the manager at the next warehouse, a large tabby cat suddenly jumped down off the manager's desk and rubbed up against Karen's legs, purring.

"Oh!" she exclaimed. "This is the first kitty I've seen here!" She stooped down to pet him, telling Rob, "I've got a cat at home. What's her name?"

Rob translated her question. "Petufina," the owner answered.

"What an unusual name!" Karen stroked her soft striped fur while the cat purred. The cat was the high point of Karen's day. She asked Rob to tell the manager that she would be back to visit, as she missed her cat in the States. The owner seemed pleased and told Karen through Rob that she was welcome anytime. Karen gave the manager a bright smile as she hugged the cat and reluctantly placed it back on the desk.

"How about lunch?" Rob asked when they were back outside. "I know a really nice place across town. Good food, and they bring a cart of salad choices right to your table."

"Oh, a real table! What, no street corner dining today?" Karen asked, poking fun at his "unbeatable burger."

He smiled. "This is, if you can believe it, even better."

They parked the jeep in front of the restaurant and walked up to the door. As they did, a small boy followed close behind them. Rob didn't appear to notice and opened the door for Karen to go first.

Upon entering, Karen's eyes swept the room in quick approval. The restaurant was equal to one of the finest in the States. Small square tables with white linen tablecloths held fresh flowers in vases and a small candle burning at each one. "Wow," murmured Karen. "This must be expensive."

Rob smiled. "No, that's one thing I like about eating here. The whole meal won't cost us over eight or nine dollars, American money."

"My treat?" Karen asked. "After all, you bought breakfast."

Rob grinned. "If you insist."

Karen was impressed as the waiter presented a pushcart of numerous varieties of salad, including three-bean, tuna, potato, cabbage vinaigrette, marinated mushrooms, even deviled eggs. She chose several items from the cart, but after studying the menu for several minutes, had no idea what else to order.

"What's *chivo*?" she asked Rob.

"Goat," he answered.

She grimaced. "Oooh, they're too much like pets. I don't think I could ever eat one."

He smiled. "You might want to try it sometime. It's very tasty."

Karen didn't think so and chose *arroz con pollo*-- chicken with rice--while Rob ordered pork chops. She thoroughly enjoyed the meal and, especially, her time with Rob, and was sorry when it was time to leave. Karen asked for the bill and successfully paid the waiter without Rob's help in figuring out the currency.

Rob grinned. "You're starting to understand the money a little. This is good practice for you--I should let you buy me lunch more often!"

Karen smiled back at him. As they left the building, she noticed that the boy was again at their heels. "What does he want?" she asked.

"I think he wants money for watching the jeep," Rob told her. "But I didn't agree to it beforehand, and I'm not going to pay him now."

"Watch for *what*?" Karen wanted to know.

"Keep it safe from being vandalized. You always wonder, though, if he's got an older brother in the shadows just waiting to rob you if you don't pay his kid brother!"

The young boy followed Rob around to the driver's side and waited until Rob got in. He placed his little hands flat against the side of the jeep, and his haunting dark eyes pleaded.

They drove off in silence. Karen felt badly that the boy was so poor he had to "watch cars" for a living. But some little boys begged--at least this one was willing to work for his pay.

"Now he'll probably grow up hating gringos," Rob muttered. "I hate that."

Karen nodded. "At least he wasn't begging."

"There were almost tears in his eyes," Rob said quietly.

Karen winced. She wished they had some reason to go back to the restaurant, then hire him to watch the jeep. If only....

Rob's voice broke into her thoughts. "We might have to go back later on. There's an art gallery across the street I want to look at."

"Me, too!" Karen agreed, grinning at him, though she hadn't known about the gallery.

He looked over at her then, and they both broke out laughing.

An hour later, after picking up a few things at the only large, air-conditioned supermarket in the city, they drove to the gallery across from the restaurant.

"There he is," Karen shouted. "Down the side street! Turn around!"

Rob turned the jeep around and drove down the side street. They parked in front of where the boy played jacks alone on the sidewalk. As they stepped out the boy watched them, recognition in his eyes.

Rob motioned for him to come over. He spoke a few words to him in Spanish, and the boy nodded eagerly. With a big grin on his face, he stood protectively near the jeep.

Karen was touched at the sight. "Why isn't he in school?" she asked Rob as they walked to the gallery. She had seen many children in their blue-and-white school uniforms crossing the city streets.

"School costs money," Rob said flatly. "The poor don't always go."

"Oh." Karen was shaken. School should be a right, not a privilege. In the States even the poorest child received an education. How could the Columbian family afford to go to school if this boy couldn't?

Karen was quiet as they viewed the walls of Venezuelan art. Rob had obviously been there before. "Here's my favorite," he told her. The painting was of a small Venezuelan village, with houses on either side of the narrow street. A small child played a game on the sidewalk out front, and a beautiful tree stood tall behind one house. Karen agreed it was a true work of art. She pointed out another, a large, vivid black and red classic that depicted a bull fight. Other paintings were much like in the States, featuring boats in a harbor or a city skyline at night. After leaving the art gallery they visited a nearby basket shop. When they finally returned to the jeep, the boy appeared out of nowhere, grinning broadly. Rob took a large coin from his pocket and paid the boy, who turned it over in his hand with a smile.

"*Momentico*," Rob said. He unlocked the jeep and took out a carton of milk, handing it to the boy along with a loaf of bread.

"*Gracias, Señor*," the boy said, and ran off happily down the street.

Rob's eyes watered. "Well," he said huskily. "We'd better go. We'll have just time to swing by the post office, then head back in time to serve supper."

She nodded. What a big heart he had! She couldn't imagine Jeff having done such a thing. But then, why was she comparing him to Jeff at all?

At the post office Karen was pleased to find a letter addressed to herself, in a childlike scrawl. Even before getting in the jeep, she ripped open the envelope and began to read. Rob watched her curiously. "More news from home?" he asked.

"Oh, Rob," she began, a smile on her face, "it's from one of the little girls at church. All of the children in Awana club were encouraged to 'adopt' a missionary, and I'm hers!"

Rob grinned.

"I'm touched. I've never been 'adopted' before! I wonder what I'm supposed to do."

"What does her letter say?"

Karen silently read the primitive handwriting. "She mostly wants to know what I do here, and what the group can pray about. And if they can send money. Isn't that sweet?"

Rob's lips curved up in a smile. "My kid sister's in Awana," he told Karen. "Bertie--Roberta. She prays for me every day. So does my little brother Joey."

"That's precious," Karen said, pleased that he had chosen to share with her. "Where are your other brothers and sisters?"

"Uh, let's see. Two sisters in college, and a brother in high school. He wants to be a missionary pilot."

They continued to share about their families and their lives at home as they drove back to the school. Right after supper cleanup that evening, Karen sat down and began to answer the young girl's letter.

Dear Andrea,

Your letter came today. Thank you for adopting me as your Awana missionary! I will tell you a little about what I do.

I plan menus and help cook for about 60 students. The two kitchen maids do a lot of the cooking. I also just started helping in a good news club on Saturday for a group of very poor children up in the hills. Last week we brought homemade playdoh for the kids to play with. They loved it, as they don't have expensive toys like you and other kids in the States.

The food buyer who works with me buys all the food for the school. That is not an easy job, because the crops aren't like in Washington. Peaches and pears and blueberries don't grow here. But there are LOTS of watermelon and cantaloupe. Here they sell fresh fruits and vegetables at large outdoor markets every day. The store sells them, too, but at a much higher price. Some items we have to drive 20 miles for. Other things are right here in Rubio. There is no "one stop shopping" in this country!

I will send you pictures of the school when I can. Thanks, again, for adopting me. I can always use your prayers!

Love,
Karen

Pleased with the way her reply had turned out, she folded the letter and placed it in an envelope, adding a few colorful stickers her mother had sent. She sighed. Now to write to all of her monthly supporters! They were paying for her to be here, and she knew she needed to correspond with them. But it would be so much easier if she had the use of a computer! What was she thinking by not bringing her laptop! That she would be living in the jungle? Taking out a pencil and some colored stationery, she vowed to at least ask Mr. Birch about borrowing an electric typewriter.

* * *

Karen yawned. The alarm had not yet gone off, but she had grown so accustomed to rising at an early hour that today, on her day off, her body was alerting her to the fact that it was time to get up.

Enjoying the luxury of lying there, Karen snuggled back under the covers. Kathie would not be picking her up for another two hours. One of the staff wives had asked Karen to accompany her and her two young sons on a trip to the swimming pool. Since there was no local pool, staff members were fond of driving the fifty-minute drive to a hotel near the Columbian border. For a minimal fee, one could use the pool and deck all day long. Karen wondered absent-mindedly what Rob was doing today, and if he had ever been to *Aguas Calientes* before.

Hours later, she was thinking of little other than the hot sun beating down on her back and was grateful that Kathie had shared sunscreen with her. With her eyes closed, she lazily dozed, then, feeling a little guilty for napping while Kathie played alone with her children, glanced at the pool. Kathie looked over and smiled. "Hey there."

"Hi," she smiled back. "I'm lying here thinking about joining you."

"We have to leave in half an hour," Kathie informed her. "I promised John I'd be home in time to cook supper." She chuckled. "I hate to say this, but as good as the school's food is, he hates eating in the dining hall! After spending all day with his students, he would much rather just come home to the boys and me."

Karen smiled, sitting up. "Can't blame him for that! I'll come in for one last swim, then."

Half an hour later, with the boys dried off and dressed in dry clothing, they started for home. Kathie had driven for only ten minutes when they arrived at an *alcabala*. There were many of the military checkpoints in the country, and so close to the Columbian border, armed guards stood ready to confront any trouble they might encounter. Karen had seen numerous *alcabalas*, but today the men looked more solemn than usual. To her dismay, rather than just waving them on, the guard motioned for Kathie to stop the car.

Unnerved, Karen said, "Why would they want us to stop?"

Kathie, apparently not worried, replied, "Oh, it could be any little thing. Probably just want to check our passports." Relieved, Karen tried to relax. Fortunately, she had heeded everyone's advice to carry her passport at all times.

Kathie stopped and rolled down her window. As the guard approached, he glanced cautiously in the back seat at the two boys, both asleep. He grunted something in Spanish, and Kathie replied with a question in her voice.

After the guard responded, Kathie turned to Karen and said calmly, "He wants us to get out of the car."

"Get out of the car--but--"

"It's okay," Kathie said, forcing a smile. "They have a lot of trouble this close to Columbia. With drugs and such. Just do what they say. I'm just sorry I have to wake the boys up."

Within minutes the four of them were out of the car and standing on the side of the road. One guard stood staring at them unabashedly as another searched the entire vehicle, even lifting up the material in the back to check the area around the spare tire.

When he had finished, one guard uttered more words in Spanish, then gave Karen an ingratiating smile and tipped his hat. Kathie buckled the boys in their seats, then climbed in behind the wheel. By the time they were on the road again, Karen realized that she was shaking. She glanced over at Kathie, who was as calm as before, and asked, "Didn't that bother you?"

Kathie laughed. "Actually, not really, I'm used to it. Just wait until you go on a trip with Kelly and Amanda and the other singles."

"What do you mean?"

"The guards like American women, especially pretty ones. Sometimes it seems like they stop the vehicle just to gawk. We always tell the single women, 'don't make eye contact'!"

Karen remembered what Rob had told her about being "white, blonde, and pretty." In spite of herself, she had to laugh.

CHAPTER SIX

Thanksgiving

Karen reviewed the Thanksgiving menu one more time. How could she possibly get all this done? The spread was as complete as a restaurant's all-you-can-eat buffet.

"Who made up the menu, anyway?" she asked Rob, who was busy emptying flour into the large bin.

"Paul Birch," he answered.

"I might have known a *man* would make up the menu," Karen sputtered. "Does he have any idea how much work this is?"

Rob looked up in surprise. "Now, wait a minute--the school features Thanksgiving dinner every year. Everyone looks forward to it because it's so traditionally American. Parents are invited, Venezuelan friends--it's really a big deal."

"That's what I mean," Karen sighed. "Turkey, dressing, mashed potatoes, gravy, rolls.... I mean, would we have to have sweet potatoes AND mashed potatoes? There's no way we can have all of this hot and on the table for two hundred people!"

Rob seemed to fight back a smile. "Hey, where's your sense of adventure? A few all-nighters in the kitchen ought to do it!"

Karen glanced over at him in shock, only to see him laughing. "No, *seriously*, Rob," she said.

Rob walked over to where she sat at the counter, threw his leg over a stool and sat down. "Okay Karen, listen. For one thing, it's really *not* as bad as it sounds. Yes, it's a lot of food. But everyone helps, not just the two of us. No one expects you to do this alone. The maids prepare a lot of it, of course, and all of the staff wives will sign up to make pies. Not a single pie comes out of this kitchen."

Karen brightened. "Really?"

Rob went down the list one item at a time. "Turkeys are hard to find--in fact, I was going to start looking next week. We can usually get them from the German butcher--imported from Columbia. Rosalba and Lucy will cook the turkeys a week ahead and I'll cut the meat off with the electric knife. All you have to do is freeze it properly."

Karen nodded.

"We do bake one turkey the day before and serve it last--that way if we have leftovers to freeze, none of the already-frozen meat gets refrozen. That's stuff we always have to think about."

He went on. "Now the office secretary, bless her heart, usually makes ALL of the stuffing. She says it's just as easy to do it all at once, and that way she doesn't have to make pies!"

Karen giggled. "Makes sense!"

"Mashed potatoes are easy. The maids will peel the potatoes the day before and store them in cold water. On Thanksgiving morning they're boiled, then Mel usually comes in and helps mash and serve."

"Wow." Karen was amazed. "It really *is* a team project!"

"Yes, it is," Rob agreed. "Last year, I was feeling pressured the same as you. I wasn't in charge of it, but I was wondering how the cook was going to pull it all together. In fact, I was still wondering an hour before we served! That last hour is kind of a blur. The kitchen came alive, it seemed like there were about fifty people in here at once, and then, PRESTO, the meal was on the table!"

Karen laughed so hard the maids turned to glance at her.

Rob continued. "Let's see.... Okay, gravy, don't worry about. Lois makes gravy a day ahead. Last year we had *lots* left. Sweet potato casserole... the only difficult thing there is, we can't always get marshmallows. Mel's wife makes them out of sugar, so ask her about that. I'll try to find them in the store, though. The maids will peel and mash the sweet potatoes a day ahead--Thanksgiving day we'll just bake."

Karen looked at the list. "And green beans are easy--Señor Mantilla always brings in plenty from his garden. We can work them up ahead."

"Jello salad--assign Rosalba to that, unless you want to do them yourself. Rolls Lucy makes ahead and freezes. They're not as fresh that way, but it works well, and they reheat with a nice golden brown crust. On Thanksgiving day you'll already be using all three of the kitchen's ovens and borrowing Roxie's upstairs in the dorm and maybe your own, so you don't want to be baking at the last minute. The maids also make the relish plates ahead--you know, pickles, celery, hot peppers."

"Hot peppers!"

"Sure, the kids love them."

"Isn't there anything I get to do?" Karen laughed.

"Yes," Rob admitted. "You can take any of those 'make-ahead' areas you're comfortable with--what you don't do, assign to a maid. Remember, the two of them have been doing this for over ten years! You also get to coordinate it all. Even though these people 'usually' do that certain item, don't assume they will this year. Ask them ahead of time, keep a good list, and check back with people. They'll come to the kitchen for ingredients, so make a shopping list for me and be sure we have plenty of whatever they need."

"Whew!" Karen's head was spinning, but she was beginning to relax a little. Cooking was a problem; coordination she could handle. With God's help, the school would have a Thanksgiving meal like all the other years.

"You can also do butterballs the day before, and dishes of jam. Do absolutely *everything* ahead that you can. And," he went on, "remember one very important thing."

"What's that?" Karen asked.

He leaned down close and whispered, "You're not in this alone, kiddo." With one swift move he was off the stool and out the door. "Gotta go, see you later." Karen sat dreamily on the stool for a minute longer. Rob's masculine scent lingered in the air, and she pondered his words. *Not alone.* Did he mean that she had *him*, or God? Still wondering, she slowly got up and walked to her room for more writing paper.

* * *

"Now remember," Roxie reminded her a few days later, "the kitchen doesn't have enough dishes for two hundred people. You'll need to borrow from the staff. Take inventory of all the kitchen utensils, plates, and cups. What you're lacking, ask for at prayer meeting next Wednesday night and the staff will bring over theirs. Whatever they supply will have to be run through the kitchen's large power washer, though-- regulations."

"I'm so glad you're here to help me." Karen smiled at her friend. "I'm a little nervous about this--Rob made it sound as though it all just 'comes together'--but I can see it's still a lot of work!"

Roxie reached over and squeezed her hand. "Yes, it is, but you'll do just fine. It sounds like you and Rob have things under control." She glanced at her watch. "I've got to go. The girls will be getting out of class any minute and I have to get a snack ready for them."

Their time together was in snatches, squeezed in between the kitchen's demanding schedule and Roxie being dorm mother to twelve junior-high girls. Karen sighed. At least she had a friend. It was just like at home--many acquaintances, but one or two true friends. Speaking of which, she remembered the letter on the bedroom dresser from her friend and former co-worker Nancy. Rob had brought it back from the city and there had been no time to read it before lunch. She walked hurriedly to her room and settled down at her desk with a cup of coffee, gently unfolding the neatly typed pages.

Karen,

You won't BELIEVE what happened at the office last week! The whole thing is changed around. We no longer HAVE a typing pool. Everyone has been assigned to one or more lawyers as personal secretary. I thought I wouldn't like it, but it's really not too bad. I got assigned to Jonesey (with some influencing on both sides!). He wanted me because I've done corporate work before. Shelly got assigned to Fred and Roz. We all think she has it the worst, but she likes litigation so she's fine with it. Basically, everyone got what they wanted! They interviewed the lawyers AND they interviewed the staff to see how it would all come out. Charlene was in the middle and told us later that everyone on both sides is happy.

I don't know where that puts you when you come back, since you were the pool supervisor. I suppose you'll be used wherever we need you. But don't worry-- they wouldn't just leave you out in the cold. And who knows--maybe by then John and I will be successful at having a baby and you can have MY job and work for Jonesey!

Karen was stunned. First Jeff and now this--her job was gone, dissolved. She felt certain Charlene would write eventually...and June was a long way off. But where did she fit into this new arrangement? The rest of

Nancy's letter was filled with anecdotes about the staff, how the city had experienced a minor earthquake, and how Nancy had frosted her hair again.

Karen clutched the letter in her hands and flopped down onto her bed. "God," she prayed, "Help me not to worry. But right now, it feels like I don't *have* a place. I don't really fit in here yet--I'm just beginning to feel at home. And I don't have a job in the States. Please continue to work in me and show me where you want me." Then, remembering Paul Birch's words once again she added, "And help me to be ready for whatever You have in store for me." She would just have to trust God for the future.

She surprised herself by not giving in to the tears that threatened. Still a tad homesick, she fought tears a lot and after a long day usually became absorbed in a good novel. The school library boasted many of the new Christian fiction books, and it was easier to lose herself in someone else's world than to deal with her own. With that in mind, she walked over to the library to check out a few more before school closed for the day.

As Thanksgiving week grew near, the high school girls were buzzing with plans of what to wear for the special occasion. This started Karen thinking. "Roxie, I'd like a new dress for Thanksgiving," she said to her friend one morning. "I haven't had time to dress shop in San Cristobal, and I've seen what the stores in Rubio carry. They're all so--so Venezuelan--you know?"

Roxie laughed. "I know just what you mean. We all have the same complaint. Have you considered having one made?"

Karen blinked. "Make one? I haven't sewn since high school, and then I couldn't do anything more complicated than a straight line!"

Roxie chuckled. "No, I mean have someone else sew one for you. There are several good seamstresses right here in Rubio. You just pick out the fabric and show them a picture of what you want. They'll measure you and make the dress just like the picture."

"You're kidding!"

Roxie smiled. "No, I'm not. It's not expensive, either, like you'd think. It costs more than the stores, but still less than you'd pay in the States! How about it? Do you want me to introduce you to *my* seamstress?"

"Yes, that would be great!"

"What about right after lunch? We'd have two hours before classes get out. I could take you then. In the meantime, I've got several clothing catalogs upstairs for you to choose a style. Today we'll just go talk to her, though."

Karen was amazed as they visited the seamstress. The woman showed them other dresses she was working on but said she would still have plenty of time if Karen brought her the fabric right away. As Roxie and the woman, obviously friends, had a conversation in animated Spanish, Karen walked around the woman's home. One area, with a separate entrance, had been set up for her sewing business. Karen was in awe at the large square opening in the roof of the hallway. Tropical plants filled the center of the room, replenished by the occasional shower and bathed in the sunshine. It was like walking through a greenhouse.

After looking through several catalogs, Karen had found a dress that would be perfect. The style was simple but pretty and would be flattering to her figure. If only she could find just the right fabric.

Roxie took her shopping in downtown Rubio on Karen's very next day off, and Karen did find just the right material. Jubilant, she asked Roxie if they could go straight over to the seamstress.

The seamstress looked at the fabric and the dress and smiled. "*Ah, qué bonita!*"

"She thinks it will be very pretty," Roxie explained, smiling.

"And there's no problem having it done by Thanksgiving?" Karen asked. "Say, the Tuesday before?"

Roxie spoke to the woman in Spanish. "No problem," she informed Karen. She explained on the way home that, though the South Americans were lackadaisical about some things, the woman knew she would not get paid for the dress unless it was done on time. And she liked to get paid! Karen floated on a cloud the rest of the day.

The Tuesday before Thanksgiving, Roxie again took Karen over to the woman's home. Karen noticed her dress as soon as she entered. The finished product was exactly the same as the one in the catalog, except for the fabric. The pretty floral print dress had a simple bodice and smooth lines, and Karen knew immediately she had made the right choice.

"You like?" asked the seamstress.

Karen beamed. "I like it very much!" she told the woman, and Roxie urged her to try it on. Karen disappeared, then re-entered the room wearing the dress and immediately received both women's approval. Karen was so pleased that she not only paid the woman but gave her a hefty tip as well.

"It *is* beautiful," Roxie told her on the way home. "A good choice. Though I know you're dying to wear it, you might consider wearing something you can get dirty for most of the day, then changing clothes about an hour before the Thanksgiving meal is served. That way you'll be a whole lot fresher."

Reluctantly, Karen had to admit she was right. She hung the dress on a hanger and was content to gaze at it for the next two days.

Thanksgiving morning quickly became a reality. Karen had her alarm set for five-thirty, and when she walked into the kitchen at six-fifteen Rob was already there.

"Good morning," Rob said brightly.

"How can you be so cheery this early in the morning?" Karen asked, suppressing a yawn.

"My one fault," he joked, and poured her a cup of coffee. "I'm cheerful 24 hours a day. Besides, I've already had my first cup of coffee!" He paused, handing the cup to her. "Are you ready for this?"

"I think so. I guess by now it's either sink or swim, huh?"

He nodded. "Since you're here, let's go over the list. The high school girls will come early to set the tables--maids will be here in an hour. So, we have some time to plan." He said suddenly, "Shall we pray?"

Karen nodded.

Rob unexpectedly took her hand and led in prayer. "Dear Father, we dedicate this day to You. We pray that the day will honor You and that we'll remember to be thankful for all You have done for us. I ask that the meal will go smoothly, and that Karen won't be nervous. This is her first time, and I pray that You will help her to relax and enjoy it even though it's a lot of work."

Karen's heart warmed as she listened to the deep voice praying for *her*, but she had a hard time concentrating on anything but how tightly Rob was holding her hand.

"We pray for our families in the States, that they'll have a good Thanksgiving without us. Bless them, Lord, and keep them safe. Help us not to be homesick. And Lord," he suddenly added, "thank You for bringing Karen this year to help us. I pray that You will continue to show her where You want her to be. Amen."

Karen was surprised to find that her eyes were filled with tears. She raised her head and looked silently over at Rob.

He squeezed her hand. "You okay?"

She nodded.

"Just a wee bit homesick?"

Karen hesitated. It would have been simpler just to agree, but she had to admit the tears were more of gratitude than homesickness. "Yes, and--and I'm just glad *you're* here, Rob," she told him. "I sure couldn't do this without you!"

"Ditto, kid," he said in a deep voice.

His face was so close to hers it made her head swim. She squeezed his hand, then reluctantly withdrew her own and picked up her coffee cup. "Okay," she said. "I'm ready."

After reviewing their list once again, they set to work. Karen walked into the big refrigerator and gazed at all of the pies, cut-up turkey, bowls of potatoes, sweet potato casserole, and Jello salads. Rob removed the large roasting pans to put into the oven. When the maids arrived, after a quick "*buenos dias*" they bustled about without supervision, as though they had the routine memorized ("They *do*, Rob reminded her!"). Karen sighed a happy sigh. How rewarding it was to see the fruit of all their labor for the past several weeks!

The day proceeded quickly. An hour before the meal, Karen walked over to her apartment to change clothes and freshen her make-up. When she returned wearing the new peach and turquoise flowered dress that just seemed to capture the golden highlights of her blonde hair, Rob's gaze followed her. He let out a low whistle that caused the maids to giggle. Karen blushed. The maids clucked in approval as Karen walked into the room. "*Muy bonita*," said Rosalba. Lucy nodded. Rob had changed clothes, too, and was strikingly handsome in a short-sleeved tan shirt and tie with dark dress pants.

All of the ovens were filled to capacity, with large trays of cooked turkey and pans of sweet potato casserole. Roxie took the rolls upstairs to heat in her own oven. Green beans and gravy bubbled in separate containers on the stove. As promised, Mel, the quiet, dependable math teacher, arrived to mash the potatoes. A visiting high-schooler's mother came early and offered to slice the pies.

Jill bristled in half an hour before serving. "Do you have an extra oven?" she said, carrying a large metal pan filled with stuffing.

Karen laughed. "You've got to be kidding! No, I don't have an 'extra' oven, but set it here. I'll take it to my apartment."

"It's hot," Jill explained. "It just needs to *stay* hot."

The entire school had rallied together for the occasion. High school girls carried plates of butterballs and dishes of jam to the tables, as well as salt and pepper and napkins. Grade school children had made table decorations and a special bulletin board with construction paper turkeys and pilgrims. Older boys had set up extra tables and moved in more chairs.

"Half an hour to go," Rob called out.

Karen glanced over at him, and he gave her a smile that sent her heart soaring.

The next half hour was a blur. Schoolchildren arrived, eager to introduce her to their parents.

"Aunt Karen, this is my mom and dad," said a grade-schooler she was fond of.

"My son says you make deviled eggs," said one mother. "I make those at home."

"My high schooler really likes the food," said another. "With us in the jungle, it's nice not to have to worry about what our kids are eating!"

Karen was deeply touched. This was God's blessing on her efforts, and she remembered all of the times in the last two months when she had felt so inadequate. She was glad she had heeded Rob's advice not to assign herself too much to do this last day. "You'll be busy supervising and playing hostess," he had advised. She was grateful for his guidance. Instead of being hot, tired, and frazzled just before serving, she was able to greet parents and hug the children with a smile on her face.

Everyone was, at last, seated, and Paul Birch prayed a grateful prayer of thanksgiving. At the last minute, with many helping hands, everything came out of the ovens. Karen dished sweet potato casserole into large bowls. The servers, high school boys, carried the hot bowls to the tables. At last, when everything was set, Karen and Rob sat down at a table filled with other staff while the maids remained in the kitchen.

"Good job, Karen and Rob," said Paul, and the others heartily agreed. Karen was still in a daze that everything had happened so quickly but remembered to smile at the blur of faces around the room.

Rob was handing her a plate. "Turkey, Karen?"

"You bet," she said, realizing that, except for that first breakfast, this was the only time she had actually shared a meal with Rob on school grounds. She gave him a warm smile and began to eat her dinner, a song of thanksgiving in her heart.

The meal was delicious, and Karen savored each item. The sweet potatoes, usually her favorite, this year took second place to Jill's stuffing. Considering another helping, Karen instead decided to proceed to pie and coffee. Hopefully the stuffing would still be available tomorrow for leftovers!

Karen wandered up to the pie table just as Rob did. She was amazed at the assortment, which included strawberry, cheesecake, lemon meringue, and of course the traditional pumpkin. "Hmmmm. They all look yummy, don't they?" she asked. "And the best part is, you and I didn't have to make a single *one* of them!"

Rob grinned over at her as he reached for a slice of pumpkin pie. "This is my second piece. Try Lois's coconut cream, it's great!"

When she was seated again, Lois Birch, sitting at the same table, asked, "Karen, are you going to the Student Government Fair this afternoon?"

"You mean, like I'll really have time to do anything else today but deal with Thanksgiving dinner?" she replied, answering Lois's question with one of her own. She took a bite of her cheesecake and smiled mischievously.

Lois grinned over at her sympathetically. "Cleanup will go faster than you think. I hope you can go--it's really a lot of fun."

Karen knew that the students had been working for weeks on their plans. Since most of the parents had come to visit at Thanksgiving, and some local guests as well, the students intended to capitalize on it! The fair would contain many booths, some selling brownies, popcorn balls, and lemonade, and even a concession stand with hot dogs and other snacks for the baseball game later that evening. The younger children were sponsoring a fish tank and a face painting booth, while the older ones had a dunk tank, a bowling game, even Bingo. All of the proceeds would go for their own student activities throughout the year. The seniors, especially, were eager to earn money, for tradition dictated that they all go on a "sneak" trip sometime before graduation.

"I volunteered to be dunked," Rob informed her. "It seemed like a good way to cool off."

Karen laughed. "How much will I have to pay to dunk you?'

"Come and find out," he said mysteriously, and she knew she had just found her reason to go.

Lois was right. After an hour and a half of organized cleanup with many hands helping, including Lois, Rob and Karen had the rest of the day off from the kitchen. Since the concession stand was offering hot dogs, corn dogs, hamburgers, even nachos, the kitchen would have been in competition. Families were on their own for any other meals that day.

Bidding Rob goodbye to report to his duties at the dunk tank, Karen quickly walked down the hall to her room to change clothes. Feeling much more comfortable again in jeans and a T-shirt, she leisurely walked the two blocks to the Boys' Dorm where the fair was being held.

"Aunt Karen, want your face painted?" a young girl asked her, and Karen laughed but politely refused. She had made it halfway down one side of the line of booths when she was suddenly grabbed by two pre-teen boys, each taking an arm.

"Hey--what's the idea?" she asked.

"Ma'am, you're going to jail," answered the short one with red hair, whom she knew only as "Tim".

"Jail? But--" she sputtered, then decided to wait and see what was going on.

Karen soon realized that the "jail" was in actuality the living room of the boys' dorm where a "guard" stood present at all times. "But--but," she stammered, "why are you putting me in jail?" She had never heard of this tradition and didn't quite know what to make of it. Her two bodyguards let go of her and disappeared, and the solemn guard standing nearby ignored her pleas.

Just then Rob walked by and waved at her through the window. She waved frantically back and began to open her mouth to shout at him.

"There's your accuser," said the boy standing guard, indicating Rob. "He has accused you of...let's see.... It's all here in the record." He consulted a piece of paper with scrawled writing on it. "Oh yes. 'Flirting.'"

"What! But that's ridic--" her mind whirled. "How long do I have to stay here?"

"Until *we* say otherwise," said the guard. "Or until your accuser drops the charges. Of course," he said in a low voice, "I could be *persuaded* to...."

"Oh. Of course." The light was beginning to dawn. "And just how much would it cost me to *persuade* you?" asked Karen.

The boy shrugged. "It would definitely have to be worth our while."

Karen fumbled in her pockets for the money she had brought. "Uh-- how about two B's?"

He shook his head. "No way. Your accuser paid us more than that to have you arrested."

"Rob--he--he *paid* to have me arrested?" she muttered, shaking her head in disbelief. "Well, I'll be. So you make money both ways!"

Within minutes she was joined by Amanda, the first-grade teacher, whose roommate, Cathy, had also had her "arrested".

"What was your offense?" Karen asked.

"I snore!" Amanda said, her ever-smiling blue eyes twinkling. "At least that's what my roommate claims. Says it keeps her awake at night. What did *you* do?"

"Nothing," Karen replied, embarrassed.

Amanda narrowed her eyes. "C'mon, Karen, *give*. They don't arrest people for 'nothing.'"

"Okay, okay. For flirting, supposedly. Rob was my accuser. But just wait until I get out of here--I'm going to get him back, believe me!"

The two girls discussed their predicament. "I didn't bring any money with me," Amanda told her. "I'm doing face painting at my first graders' booth and figured I wouldn't have time to do much else. But my booth's not making any money with me sitting in here!"

The guard appeared not to hear.

"Suppose we break out of here?" said Karen in a loud whisper, watching the guard's face.

"I wouldn't do that if I were you, ma'am," the boy said in an ominous tone. "The penalties are heavier in foreign countries, you know. Besides," he said, glancing at his watch, "your time's up. Your accuser said ten minutes unless you paid first. He figured you'd pay."

"You mean I can go?"

"You can go."

"But what about my friend here?" Karen asked.

"What about her?" The junior high boy was definitely enjoying playing the tough guy.

"How long is she in for?"

"Fifteen minutes."

Karen considered, then handed the boy a foreign bill. "Will this get her out early?"

The guard smiled, then pocketed the money. "Yes, ma'am. And good day to you both."

The girls burst out laughing, then ran through the door before the guard could change his mind. "Just wait until I find Rob--" Karen began, as Amanda hurried away.

"Oh, Karen, thanks!" Amanda called out with a smile. "Come by my booth and I'll paint your face for free!"

Karen had soon located the dunk tank and watched as Paul Birch made a big splash in the water. Evidently Rob was up next, for he stood just at the side ready to climb inside. Karen caught his eye, then crossed her arms over her chest and did her best to look angry.

Rob gave her a disarming wink and looked away. Paul gave up his spot and Rob climbed inside the tank. After buying a ticket, Karen eagerly took her place in line beside several others. All of them missed, and when it was Karen's turn Rob cockily announced, "Come on, I dare you--if a man couldn't do it, I certainly don't expect a woman to!"

Karen took that as a personal challenge. Pulling back her arm, she threw--hard.

The first ball missed.

The second, third and fourth balls also missed. The bystanders were obviously disappointed, and a couple of high school guys went to buy more tickets.

Karen drew back her arm and threw the fifth ball. With a yell and a splash, Rob dropped into the cold water. Everyone clapped, and as Rob surfaced, she shot him a triumphant glance.

Feeling pleased with herself, Karen sauntered over to the face-painting booth. To show her school spirit, she let Amanda paint her face but insisted on paying for it. "After all, the money's for the kids," Karen told her.

"Hey--the group's going out for ice cream after the game," Amanda said as she added a tiny flower to Karen's cheek. "Would you like to go with us?"

"The group?"

"Yeah--Cathy and I, and Kelly and Jennifer. I think Pete and Rob are going, too. We're in a classroom so much we kind of want a *break* from the kids," she told Karen in a hushed voice, so not to hurt the children's feelings. "How 'bout it?"

Karen was pleased to be asked. When the baseball game was over that evening, the seven singles piled into Rob's jeep, Joe in the front next to Rob and the girls in the middle and back. The local ice cream parlor featured flavors and combinations of all kinds, though Karen had to have most of them explained to her because of the funny Spanish titles. Karen had never been with Rob in a group situation, and noticed how different it was from the easy comraderie they shared between just the two of them! She was quick to observe that, after Rob's initial teasing, asking her if her arm hurt by so much throwing, he was careful to include everyone in the group as they conversed easily with one another. Within the group Karen felt almost shy around him and focused instead on getting to know the others a little better. Pete, a quiet man who taught science, was even more shy around so many single women. He grinned at Rob's ribbing and seemed to enjoy the girls' teasing as well. Karen noticed that Amanda wasn't her usually bubbly self but seemed intent on asking Pete questions and drawing him out of his shell. Jennifer reminded Karen of a co-worker back home, beautiful and quick-witted, with long dark hair almost to the waist. Blonde, short-haired Cathy was quiet and intelligent, and seemed to know a little something about everything. Kelly, with her easy-cut hairstyle and quiet manner, was friendly but guarded, and Karen could tell she took her teaching responsibilities at the school very seriously.

Karen thoroughly enjoyed the entire weekend. The following day was full with parent-teacher conferences in the morning and an afternoon of track and field competition. She and Rob had planned an outdoor lunch, with submarine sandwiches, chips, and brownies, and the weather cooperated fully. That evening the high schoolers put on a play for those who had purchased a ticket, a South American rendition of a comedy Karen had seen in the States.

On Saturday most of the parents started for home, and by Sunday the campus was back to just students and staff. By Sunday night Karen realized that, though the weekend was fun and exciting, it had taken its toll. Classes began again the next day for the students, but Karen was grateful that Monday was her day off, to do absolutely nothing if she chose!

CHAPTER SEVEN

Christmas in a Faraway Place

O
h no!" Karen exclaimed. "The jar broke!" She
had placed the large glass jar of maple syrup in
a kettle of water to melt the big lump of sugar
that had crystallized in the bottom. The students
were due for breakfast in fifteen minutes.

Rob was his usual calm self. "Go ahead and make
some real quick," he suggested.

"*Make* some?"

"Sure--here, come flip these, and I'll do it." He
gave her the pancake turner and bustled around the
kitchen gathering ingredients. She watched as he
poured water into a pan, added lots of sugar, and
stirred. She flipped the pancakes, then watched him add
a few teaspoons of maple flavoring.

"Fifteen minutes," he muttered. "Just long enough.
Trade me places again."

She calmly did as he said. He poured more batter
onto the griddle, and she took his place at the stove.

"Let it come to a boil but keep stirring."

Karen smiled at him gratefully. "I'm sure glad *you* know what you're doing."

"It happened last year," Rob admitted, but he looked pleased at her compliment. "The other cook did the same thing then, or I wouldn't have known. The maids use a more refined method, but it turns out almost the same. Mine might be a little watery."

Karen was amazed at how much she was learning. To her, cooking had never been a great love--she thought it would be the supervisory part of this job she would enjoy. But as she watched the maids work, and prepared breakfast and supper each day with Rob, she became more and more interested in creating some dishes on her own.

One day Rob had returned from market, and she spied some large green avocados on a crate. "What are those for?" she asked. "Don't tell me you're going to make your own 'unbeatable burgers.'"

"Guacamole!" he said triumphantly. "For tacos tonight. Whatdya think?"

"Sounds great! Do you know how to make it?"

"No, but there's a good American cookbook on the counter. Would you like to help me experiment?"

Karen eagerly grabbed the large book and scanned the table of contents for a recipe. For the next half hour they peeled, chopped, mashed, and stirred. The maids, flipping homemade tortillas on the large grill, watched the two curiously.

"It's just like the Mexican restaurants!" Karen exclaimed. "Do the kids like it?"

"I don't know," Rob admitted. "I don't think it's been served here before, at least not recently. Avocados are usually kind of expensive, but sometimes I think it's worth it to go the extra mile to make the kids feel at home."

He gave the maids a taste. "Hmm," they nodded knowingly, "*guasacaca*."

"*Guasacaca*?" Karen repeated.

"*Si,*" clucked Rosalba, and began telling Rob in Spanish that the dish had been served a couple years before, and the students very much liked it then.

By the time the meal was over it was obvious they still did. Not a bit of the green concoction remained.

"That was a good idea!" Karen told Rob as they wrapped leftovers and put them away.

Rob winked. "Yeah. We make a good team."

Karen blinked. Yes, they *did* make a good team. It was too bad she would just be getting used to working with him and it would be time for her to go....

"Yes," she said out loud, "we do at that. Well, I'm getting out of here. See you bright and early." She walked across the hall to her apartment, as Rob gazed after her in silence.

Two days later Rob asked her, "Karen, do you think you could handle supper alone on Friday, two weeks from tomorrow?"

"Sure--supper's no problem," Karen told him. She was used to it, since often his marketing trips to San Cristobal ran late. "Are you going on a buying trip?"

"Well, no--I've--I've been asked to chaperone some kids for the Christmas banquet that night. So, all you'll have for supper is dorm parents and the younger grades--probably around 30."

Karen nodded, her mind racing. Chaperone--certainly he didn't plan on going *alone* to the banquet. She wondered....

As if reading her thoughts, he added, "I've asked Kelly to help me. There'll be several couples chaperoning."

Karen forced a smile. "You don't have to explain it to me. I'll be happy to take care of supper. Maybe I'll do something special for the smaller group. Like chocolate bananas or hot fudge sundaes for dessert."

"Great. Thanks," Rob said, seeming relieved.

Karen excused herself and began dishing up butterballs for lunch. After all, why shouldn't he take Kelly? *Someone* had to stay behind and serve dinner to those remaining. And up to this point Rob had given no indication of having a special interest in Karen. His actions had always been friendly, considerate, and helpful. Besides, she reminded herself once again--she was leaving at the end of the year.

Over the next couple of weeks, Karen noticed that the easy comraderie between them was gone. The air seemed stiff, and conversation was stilted. Both Rob and she were lost in their own thoughts. The kitchen work went on as usual, but Karen found that she tired more easily and was ready to go to bed by nine-thirty each evening.

* * *

CLANG! CLANG! CLANG! CLANG! CLANG!

Karen woke with a start. The loud banging appeared to be coming from just outside the window. She wondered if an emergency had arisen and someone was banging the locked gates of the school, trying to get someone's attention. Peering out between the curtains, she saw a boy, probably no older than ten or eleven, banging a metal pipe on a nearby lamppost.

"What the--" Karen wondered if she should call Roxie's husband Joe. Besides being the dorm father, he was also the school's night watchman. Maybe the boy needed help! He must be homeless, or why else would he be on the street at such an hour? Glancing at the clock, she noticed that it was four a.m.! Well, she reasoned, this could be an emergency.

Joe answered the phone with a very sleepy "Hello". After Karen explained the situation, Joe only chuckled. "Karen, go back to sleep--if that's possible. I'll explain in the morning. Much *later* morning. And Karen--"

"Yes?"

"Don't worry about the kid."

But Karen couldn't help be concerned. It seemed like hours before the banging finally stopped. After another fitful hour or two of sleep, she got up, showered and dressed, then made her way to the kitchen. When Rob arrived ten minutes later, she poured him a cup of coffee and told him about the boy.

Rob laughed, then turned on the griddle and accepted the cup from her. "Ah, yes, our dear Venezuelan customs. For twelve days before Christmas each year, the priest pays boys to bang on lampposts at 4:00 a.m. to wake people for 5:00 o'clock mass!"

Karen's mouth fell open. "You're kidding!

"No, I'm not. Practically the whole country is Roman Catholic. You and I are a minority here."

"Then why don't they leave OUR area alone?" Karen wailed. "Staff lives across the street, so there's probably no one in a two-block range of the school who's going to go to mass just because that kid woke them up!"

"Don't tell the priest that," Rob told her with a grin. "That kid would be out of a job!"

Still shaking her head, Karen added more cinnamon to the egg and milk mixture, then began dipping the slices of white homemade bread into it. Rob busied himself with spreading a thin layer of oil on the griddle. They worked silently side by side for the next half hour making the French toast. Karen longed to talk to him but couldn't think of anything to say. She was very tired from lack of sleep, but she knew it was more than that. Rob, too, looked weary and said nothing.

The Monday before the banquet, Karen took a bus to San Cristobal. She had already sent packages home to her parents and a few friends with a teacher leaving last week for the States, but still needed to buy gifts for friends here. Definitely one for Roxie, one for each member of the Birch family, who had invited her to spend Christmas with them. And, she thought ruefully, something special for Rob.

She began walking the streets looking for just the right gifts. The jewelry store had just the perfect thing for Roxie--a tiny silver replica of the map of Venezuela dangling from a silver chain. She bought a handcrafted doll and a wooden handmade truck for the Birch children, and a leather wallet for Paul Birch. She headed toward the dress shop to see what she could find for Lois Birch. Walking leisurely down the street she heard a loud wolf whistle. Ignoring it, she heard an even louder, "Hey *Gringa*!"

Recognizing the term Venezuelans used for "white woman," she turned mostly out of curiosity. To her surprise, Rob stood across the street grinning at her. She laughed. What a place to run into him!

"Hey!" he yelled. "Cross the street!"

She waited for the cars to pass, then crossed the street and walked toward him smiling. "Fancy meeting another gringo here," she teased.

His eyes twinkled. "What're *you* doing here?"

"Christmas shopping--what else? Rubio doesn't have much to offer. How about you?"

"Same. Find anything?"

"Oh, yes! I've been here since nine. I only have a couple more to get." She omitted the fact that one was his!

"Well--" Rob looked at his watch. "You'll have to wait until two o'clock now. It's noon--the stores will be closing for two hours. How about letting me buy you lunch?"

Karen flushed and shrugged. Why this sudden nervousness with him? "That'd be nice," Karen said, and they started a slow walk down the street toward his jeep. "You really don't have to pay, though--I *am* an independent working woman, you know." *Save your money for Friday night*, she was thinking, but kept the words to herself.

"That's okay," Rob said in a half-serious tone. "It would be my pleasure."

She felt her face flush again. "Where are we going?"

"Our salad place. Is that okay?"

Our salad place. She liked the sound of it. They had eaten there only twice before on buying trips, but already it was "theirs".

"That sounds super. Do you think we could stop by and look at paintings afterward?"

"If we wait until two," Rob replied, grinning. "Siesta--remember?"

Karen made the most of her two hours with Rob. After loading her packages into the jeep, they drove over to the restaurant. They both ordered salad items from the cart and roasted chicken from the menu, which Rob recommended.

"Funny," Rob said, "it seems like the only time we talk in complete sentences is when we're eating! Ever feel like our whole life revolves around food?"

"That's because it *does*," Karen admitted. "I get tired of thinking about food all the time. I'm glad break is coming up soon. Are you?"

"Yeah--*really*. What are you doing for Christmas?"

"Paul and Lois have invited me over for Christmas Day."

"Really? Me too!"

Karen's heart fluttered.

"They're very considerate," Rob went on. "It's not easy to be this far away from home at Christmas."

"It's not easy to be this far away from home even when it's not Christmas," Karen said solemnly.

Rob nodded, then studied her. "Are you having a hard time?"

Karen hesitated. She fought homesickness continually, but even more so the last couple of weeks, especially since the air had been strained between she and Rob. To speak would mean to cry, so she said nothing but looked over at him through a blurry mist and nodded.

"I'm sorry," Rob said gently. "I didn't know. This being my second year and all, I forget what it's like to be new." He briefly reached over and covered her hand with his.

"Yes, and with you being a 'lifer' and all," Karen said, finding her voice again but fighting to keep it steady.

He grunted. "A lifer, huh? I don't know about that, but I'm here for as long as God wants me here."

"Did you always feel like that?" she asked.

"Pretty much. I started out, believe it or not, with a college major in sociology. That got pretty dull after a while, though. Especially when what really matters to me is people, not theories or principles. My job allows me to be out rubbing elbows with people, using my Spanish, sometimes getting an opportunity to witness for God.

"When you're white, everyone is watching you. What you do says who you are, good or bad." He paused. "Do you miss your job in Seattle?"

Karen nodded. "My parents, too, and my cat, and my friends, but--especially my job. I would *love* to get up tomorrow morning and drive downtown to that same ten-story building and go to work without wearing an apron! I love the business world. You might not understand that, but--it's all I've known, and I was--am--good at it. There's a job waiting for me when I go back." Then she sobered, remembering the firm's recent changes. "At least, I think there is."

"Would you consider coming back here?"

"Right now, no. I'm still having a hard time getting through the *first* year. I know I'm supposed to be here, but part of what gets me through is knowing I can go home at the end of June! God would have to do a lot of work on me before I change *that* much."

"He has before, you know," Rob said softly.

"I *know*," she admitted. "Scary thought!"

They both laughed, and the conversation was light as they finished their meal and ordered *café con leche*.

"You're good, you know," he said unexpectedly.

"Good--at what?"

"The kitchen."

"The kitchen?" Karen laughed nervously. "I feel like I'm messing up all the time! Like last week when I let the meat spoil."

"The electricity was off--that wasn't your fault," Rob stated. "Things like that are to be expected here. You do just fine."

"But I can't even cook! You mean supervising?"

"I mean all of it. The maids really like you. The kids like the menus you've been serving. The school board likes the fact that you're able to stay within the budget. You've added some new foods--stuff I wouldn't have thought of. I think the kids know you care." Then he added, "And you cook better than you think you do."

Karen was deeply moved. "Thank you, Rob. I appreciate that more than you know."

His gaze was warm upon her. "Shall we go?" he asked softly. "It's almost two."

She nodded.

Rob motioned to the waiter. "*La cuenta, por favor.*" As was the Venezuelan custom, the waiter did not bring the bill until it was requested.

"Wonderful lunch," Karen told Rob as they waited, realizing as she said it that the meal was good, but the company was even better. "Thank you."

"My pleasure. Say, Karen--" he began.

"Yes?"

"Thanks for doing supper alone on Friday."

Karen tensed and was instantly sorry Rob had brought it up. She had forgotten all about *the date* and had simply enjoyed being with him. "No problem," she replied stiffly.

"The kids wanted to go to El Tama for dinner."

"Oh. But that's in Columbia, isn't it?"

"Yes, just over the border. It's a really nice place and a favorite with the high schoolers." He paused. "Too bad your visa doesn't have multiple entry. I could take you there sometime."

Karen sat for a moment, letting his words sink in. "You mean--I can't go to Columbia on my visa?"

"No--you can't cross the border even for five minutes with the type of visa you have! It's too bad because there's some good shopping over there. That's where I get several food items that can't be purchased in Venezuela."

Karen let his words sink in. Suddenly her face broke into a smile. At the same time, Rob's brown eyes twinkled at her. Without exactly *stating* it, he had told her an awful lot just then. She was grateful and very, very pleased.

The waiter came as they sat grinning at each other. Rob gave him the money and the man disappeared again.

Karen could think of nothing to say, so took another sip of her now-cold coffee. She was still basking in the thought that, *maybe*, Rob had only asked Kelly because Kelly had the right kind of visa!

Rob just smiled. The waiter brought change and they left the restaurant.

On the street again, Rob said, "Now what?"

"Well--I don't generally let men 'pick me up,'" Karen teased, "so, I suppose I ought to go finish my shopping."

"Yes, but this is the Christmas season," he teased back. "Anything can happen. Let's go shopping together. You know, since we'll both be at the Birches for Christmas, I suppose we should get each other something, too."

"I suppose so," Karen agreed, her eyes shining.

"What do you want?"

Karen thought about it. "Nothing much," she replied. "A crate of apples would be nice." She knew good and well that apples were one of the most expensive items in Venezuela. "Or even one large, red, sugary caramel apple!"

"Whew!" Rob did a double take. "A woman with 'taste'! Is that *all*?"

"No," she said seriously. "What I'd really like is a kitten. But you can't buy them here."

"No," Rob agreed. "You can't."

After visiting several shops together, Karen began wondering how she would shop for Rob's gift with him always at her side! Since visiting the painting shop once again, she was certain what she wanted to buy him. She hated to linger behind to buy the painting without his presence, though, and ride the long hot bus back to Rubio when she could enjoy Rob's company for another hour! While his back was turned, she wrote down the name and price of the painting he liked. There was still a week and a half until Christmas. If Roxie or one of the single girls couldn't give her a ride to San Cristobal again, she would just have to take the bus and go alone! After all, it was for Rob. It would have been simpler to do it today, but once her decision was made, she decided to go with it. If Rob asked her for a ride home, she would happily accept.

When Rob came into view again, Karen said, "Actually, I was just headed to the dress shop when you caught up with me. Do you think we could go there?"

Rob made a face and Karen burst out laughing.

"I mean, if it's not against your principles or anything!"

He gave her a warm smile. "Sure. Buying a Christmas dress?"

"No," she told him, heading out the door. "I'm hoping to find something for Lois. Maybe a maternity blouse or something." Rob's prediction had proven correct, and Lois had recently announced her pregnancy with their third child.

Rob chose to wait in the jeep while Karen shopped. The time was well spent, for she found a loose-fitting smock she was certain Lois would like, and a casual pair of pants for herself.

On the drive back to the school, Rob started off by singing a Christmas carol and Karen joined in. One song led to another, and before they knew it the dusty streets of Rubio had come into sight. Karen was laughing as Rob helped gather up her numerous packages. Supper was just beginning as they walked through the large dining hall to get to Karen's apartment, and many pairs of eyes followed them. Karen couldn't help wondering if Kelly was watching, too.

Christmas break was a welcome respite. The first week was totally free, with Christmas Day falling mid-week. Following that would be a week of mission conference, when all of the outreach workers in Venezuela would travel to the school to meet, plan, pray, and take care of business matters. Even the farthest ones came, so the children whose parents lived in the jungle were excited at the prospect of a family visit. With so many visitors coming, the staff was busy as they figured out hostess homes for everyone to stay in. A special staff would come in to cook so that Karen and Rob could attend all of the meetings.

The Saturday after school was out, Karen and Roxie made their weekly trip up the mountain to visit Pedro and the group. Bible club was put on hold for two weeks while conference was in session, so this was the last time to visit before January. The women had pooled their resources and bought inexpensive gifts for each child. Rob had donated money, too, and there had been enough to buy food as well: a huge bag of oranges, sacks of flour and sugar, coffee, and a bag of potatoes. Karen and Roxie had spent an afternoon baking and frosting sugar cookies out of special shapes--bells, trees, candy canes--to the children's delight. A special treat was several bottles of bubble blowing soap, a gift from Kelly's mother who had just visited from the States.

The story Roxie told that day was of baby Jesus, born in a manger, and even the parents gathered around to listen. For fifteen minutes the children colored the pictures of baby Jesus Karen had brought, then ate the cookies. Karen was glad they had made plenty, for several parents lingered and joined in the celebration. There were enough cookies for everyone to have two or three.

When gifts were passed out, the children screamed with delight. Plastic barrettes and tiny cars would have seemed cheap presents in the States, but these girls had probably never owned a store-bought hair ornament, and certainly none of the boys had a shiny toy car. Pedro walked up to Karen and showed her his little red truck, a bright smile on his face. She gathered him up in her arms and gave him a big hug as he squealed with glee. Others had warned her of picking up lice from the children, but at the moment she didn't care. This might be the only way he would know of God's love.

After club was over, Roxie and Karen waited, at Karen's insistence, to talk to Pedro's mother. "Have you ever taken him to have his ears checked?" Roxie asked her in Spanish.

Carmelina shook her head. She explained that Pedro had been deaf since an illness as a small baby. "Ask her if she would allow us to take him to a doctor," Karen prompted.

Roxie hesitated. "Maybe we should talk about this first."

"Please," Karen pleaded.

"You could be opening a can of worms," Roxie warned. "What if the doctors can't help him? And the other children have needs, too. If we help one, they'll expect help with all of them."

"I know--but at least they can hear!" Karen's eyes were moist. "Please, Roxie. We have to get him help."

Roxie softened and had a lengthy conversation with the woman. Karen could see the hope in the mother's eyes and wondered if Roxie had been right. Would she be giving this woman hope, just to let her down? Roxie turned to Karen then. "If you can help her son, she will be forever grateful."

Karen gave Carmelina a big smile and took her hand. "I'll try," she said sincerely. "I promise I'll try."

Later in the week Roxie made an appointment with a doctor in San Cristobal for the second week in February.

"Can't they do it sooner than *that*?" Karen complained.

Roxie smiled sympathetically. "We're fortunate to get in *that* early! You have to remember, everything here shuts down for a couple weeks after the first of the year. Especially in San Cristobal."

"Why?"

"Well, first it takes them a while to get going after New Year's. Then comes the *Feast of the Three Kings*, a Venezuelan holiday. They have costume parades, street dances. And, as if that isn't enough, the third week in January is *La Feria de San Sebastian*--the whole city celebrates for four days with sports, bullfights, and fairs. Seems like the whole month of January the country is celebrating something!"

Karen was impatient. But there was no other alternative, and in the meantime, she had Christmas festivities to think about. To prepare for Christmas day at the Birches, she isolated herself in the kitchen one afternoon and made two apple pies. The apples had cost her a small fortune, but she was certain her hostess would be pleased. Rob told her he was bringing fried *platanos*, a dish made from the yucca plant. Karen thought it tasted like it sounded--"yuk!" When boiled, the bland vegetable was virtually without flavor. But sliced and deep fried, Rob insisted it was very much like potato chips. Lois Birch would be preparing the traditional Venezuelan dishes: *hallacas*--banana leaves filled with tasty meat and vegetables--and *pan de jamón*--bread filled with smoked ham, olives, and raisins.

Christmas morning, Karen dressed in a festive red pantsuit and pulled her long blonde hair back in a bright Venezuelan clip. When she arrived at the Birches, she was surprised to find a whole houseful of people. Besides the Birch family there was Rob, Kelly, Cathy and Jennifer, as well as Amanda and Pete, who had recently paired off. The young people enjoyed a long day of playing table games, munching on snack foods, and singing around the piano. In the early evening they all sat down to the traditional holiday meal. Lois was an excellent cook and received many compliments. With her Venezuelan dishes and the group's contributions, including Karen's pies, the meal turned out to be a veritable feast.

When Paul suggested they gather 'round the tree for singing and gifts, Karen wasn't sure what to do. She had gifts for the Birches, and one for Rob as well. But she hadn't realized all of these people would be here, and if she gave Rob his gift it would look like he was "special". On the other hand, if she told him she would like to give him his later, he might get the wrong idea.

Rob solved the problem for her. Since there was no gift under the Christmas tree from him, Karen noticed, she decided to wait until later on and just say nothing. Since her gift was already under the tree, Karen asked Lois to discreetly put his package out of sight until Karen asked for it.

The Birch children were thrilled with the handmade gifts Karen had chosen. They thanked her shyly, and their mother prompted a hug for Karen from each of them. She had selected a smock with a flowered print for Lois, which Lois held up in delight. In return Lois had given Karen three small adobe houses, tiny replicas of the real ones Karen had seen. Karen was quick to note that the Birches had a small gift for each person in the room. She was touched that they had chosen this yearly tradition, to help newcomers and singles not feel quite so homesick in a faraway place.

Paul Birch opened the package containing the leather wallet and thanked Karen sincerely. "Now if Lois will just let me have money to go in it," he teased. The others exchanged gifts, too--Jennifer with Kelly, Cathy with Amanda. Karen glanced over at Rob. His eyes smiled at her as he met her gaze. Had he decided not to give her a gift after all?

The hour grew late, but no one seemed to be minding the time. "Well, I'd better go," Karen finally said, glancing at her watch. "I was going to try to call my parents yet tonight. It's three hours earlier in Seattle." She retrieved the package from the back room, grateful that Lois had slipped it into a sack, and thanked the Birches for a wonderful day.

Taking their cue from Karen, the other singles, too, decided to take their leave. The Birch children, dressed in pajamas, had sweet smiles and goodbyes for everyone. Karen told Lois to keep the rest of the remaining pies, then walked outside into the warm December night.

Since school was only two blocks away, Karen was not afraid to walk alone in the little village. How different that was from her hometown of Seattle! What also seemed strange was that on Christmas Day it was as warm as summertime in the States! Pete and Amanda were behind her and held hands as they strolled along. Kelly and the other two girls had driven, so Karen was alone.

"Karen, WAIT!" she heard suddenly. It was Rob. "Can I walk with you?"

"My pleasure," she said sincerely.

They walked in companionable silence for a few minutes. "Oh, uh--this is for you." Karen pulled the wrapped package out of the bag. "Since I didn't have gifts for anyone else, I wanted to wait until we were alone."

Rob seemed pleased. "Let's wait until we get to your apartment," he suggested.

Karen was puzzled but didn't object. Rob seemed ready to burst with excitement, but said nothing, only hummed along beside her. "I had a great day," he told her. "Isn't Lois a good cook?"

"She sure is."

"And your apple pie was delicious!"

"Thanks. Expensive, too, but worth it!"

"Just what I like," he joked, "a woman with taste!"

They had reached Naughton Hall, and Karen opened the front door and stepped into the sala. "Uh-- would you like to come in?" she asked awkwardly. She had not expected a guest, and the apartment was a mess of Christmas wrap, cookie decorating supplies, and unwashed dishes.

"Sure--I like to see my women in safely," he teased.

She shot him a strange look and unlocked the door of her apartment. At a sound near the window, she whirled around and gasped. There, hiding behind the long drapes, was a tiny orange striped kitten, its back arched, hissing at her!

"Oh!" She cried out in delight. "Oh, Rob!" She knew instantly the kitten was a gift from him. Laying her sweater and Rob's package on the table, she walked slowly over to the kitten, being careful not to frighten it. It hissed again, and she spoke soothingly and coaxed it closer. As the kitten grew calmer, she picked it up and petted its soft fur, nestling it under her chin. "How did it get in here?"

"I asked Roxie to keep it upstairs until just a while ago," Rob explained. "I didn't want it to be lonely. *Or* to make too big of a mess in here alone!"

"You mean it's from you? Oh, Rob, I just *love* it. Wherever did you find her?"

"*Him*. It's a boy. The warehouse manager told me of someone whose cat just had a litter," he explained, grinning. "What'll you call him?"

"Oh, I don't know. Here, please sit down." She motioned to her maroon flowered sofa and Rob sat on the edge and watched her. "Oh, Rob, I don't know what to say. Except," her voice grew soft, "thank you. Thank you, thank you, thank you!"

"You're very welcome. I knew it was what you wanted most. Besides," he said, chuckling, "it cost me a lot less than a crate of apples!"

She had a momentary panic. "Am I allowed to have a cat in here?"

"I didn't ask," said Rob, grinning. "I *would* suggest you keep him inside your apartment, though, because the school watchdog is death on cats. And don't let him in the kitchen. That could be a problem. Regulations, I mean. But here in your own place, I don't see why anyone would object."

"I'll make him a litter box," Karen planned aloud, "and give him milk at first, then tuna. Do they sell cat food in Venezuela?"

"Yes, but it's expensive. You'd be better off feeding him kitchen scraps."

She stroked the kitten's soft orange fur and listened to him purr. When the city siren went off, she realized with a start that it was midnight. And she was alone in her apartment with Rob!

"Oh! I have a present for you," she remembered suddenly, embarrassed that she had so quickly forgotten about Rob's gift. Carrying the kitten over to the sofa, she retrieved the package from the table where she had left it.

Rob pulled off the ribbon and slowly began to unwrap the gift. "My painting!" he exclaimed. "Karen, you never cease to amaze me. How did you know?"

"You told me," she reminded him. "Don't you remember?" In truth, she remembered everything Rob had ever said to her.

Rob continued to admire his painting as she stroked the kitten's fur. "Now I won't be so lonely," she told the kitten, whose hair was just the color of pumpkins. "I know--I'm going to call you 'Punkin'."

Rob grinned approvingly. He seemed reluctant to leave, and just sat watching Karen cuddle the little animal.

"Wait 'til I tell my parents!" Karen said. "Oh! My parents!" Glancing at her watch, she remembered she hadn't called them yet.

Taking that as a hint, Rob said, "Well, I suppose I'd better go."

She hugged the kitten to herself. "Thanks again, Rob. This is the best present I could have received."

His eyes, staring straight into hers, were unreadable. "Thank *you*."

They both rose and walked over to the door. At the doorway Rob hesitated, then turned and touched Karen lightly on the cheek. "Merry Christmas, Karen," he said softly, then turned and walked away, leaving only the scent of his aftershave behind.

CHAPTER EIGHT

A Visit to the Hospital

When Karen stepped onto the scale for the first time since Christmas, she was shocked. She had gained five pounds! There had to be a way to work in the kitchen and still maintain her weight. She had expected to give some things up to come to South America, but her figure had *not* been one of them! Bemoaning this fact the next day in Roxie's presence, Roxie informed her of an exercise class two days a week in the school's gymnasium.

"It's one of the school's evangelistic outreaches for the new year," Roxie explained. "Amanda teaches it. It's free, and we encourage anyone to go that wants to."

"You're kidding!" Karen was beginning to feel like this place was too good to be true. In reality, when she made the decision to come to South America for a year, she *had* thought she would be giving up a lot to do so. Maybe, she mused, that was partly due to the way the Women's Missionary Society of the church had treated her with awe. On hearing the news, they had asked her to come speak to the group about her decision. They served her lunch and asked her one question after another. And, though they didn't feel they could support her on a monthly basis, they had taken an offering and graciously awarded Karen a good sum for her travel expenses.

But in reality, Karen felt she had given up nothing to come. *Except*, she thought wryly, *Jeff, of course*. The pain lessened with time, and Karen was beginning to realize that Jeff had clearly not been the man God intended for her to marry. In some ways she wondered why she had never seen the light before. Had she been so blinded by his suave and good looks, his touch, his self-assured manner, his flattering words?

Karen sighed. Yes, she had.

Snapping back to the present, she quickly asked Roxie for details and vowed to show up as soon as the class began the week school started. Now if she could only stop sampling the baked goodies!

The next two weeks Karen kept busy with the missions conference. Training sessions were required, but business meetings were optional for short termers such as Karen, since they could not vote. Karen opted to go to most of the meetings, but also volunteered to assist Lois with games for the small children so their parents could attend. Lois was grateful for the help with so many cooped-up children, for rainy season had begun and it was pouring outside. Large drops of water pelted against the window. The weather reminded

Karen of home, and of the long, rainy Saturdays she would curl up with a good book and a cup of coffee.

"You know, Karen," Lois told her as they watched the children coloring. "I teach the Spanish classes here. Would you be interested in joining one?"

"Oh! You mean it would be okay?" Karen asked in surprise. "I thought the classes were just for the students."

Lois smiled. "They are, but a student can be any adult who is a part of the school. It would really add to your ministry here to know the language. Especially Bible club. I've heard you speak some Spanish, and you're not bad--but your vocabulary is limited. One of my classes next quarter is intermediate--I think you would fit right in."

Karen smiled. Maybe she did fit in here, after all. "I--I'd like that," she replied gratefully. "Thanks for thinking of me."

During break, Karen was pleased that she was able to get to know so many of the teachers and staff wives on a personal basis. With a few remaining days before school started, Lois Birch had asked Karen to accompany her on a trip to a small village in the hills. "There's a group of people at Cascarí I need to check on," she explained. "A Christian woman there holds a Bible club for the children every week and I meet with her, we share ideas; I also bring her pages for the children to color. She's really a marvel. Although very poor herself, she was using her own money for refreshments until I told her we would be happy to help out. She's dead set against accepting charity, but since someone at the school started the club, I told her it just wasn't right for her to support it on her own. Every week the pastor of their little church eats dinner at her house. So, I told her to save her money to feed the pastor." Lois smiled. "Since he's young and hearty, she agreed to do just that!"

Karen watched eagerly out the window as Lois drove. So, they were going to the place that Rob had mentioned. Several weeks ago, he had begun attending Sunday evening services up in the hills at Cascarí. Sunday mornings she and Rob both attended the chapel the school provided, since it was in English, and they were both needed to serve dinner within half an hour after the service ended. Many of the staff families attended local Venezuelan churches, though, and loved it.

As Karen marveled at the scenery around her, she could understand why Rob made the long drive each week. She had never seen a coffee farm before, and in the lush greenery surrounding the village, coffee thrived. Karen smiled at the sight of a large coffee cup on a pole outside one of the buildings. The sun shone brightly after last night's rain, making everything even greener and brighter and fresh smelling. Wild poinsettias were in full bloom, and even the most modest of homes was surrounded by beautiful flowers.

Once at the village of Cascarí, Lois pulled up to a small, broken-down house and stopped. After they were both out of the car, she pointed across the road to a sturdy-looking white stucco building.

"Karen, that's the building your church paid for," Lois informed her.

"What?"

"About fifteen years ago, maybe before you went there. The Cascarí church had been meeting in homes but was getting too big and desperately needed its own building. Your church in Seattle took special offerings over a period of months. The Vacation Bible School children even made it their week-long project."

Karen suddenly felt warmed from head to toe. Yes, now she remembered. *She* had been one of those children, and she had brought her pennies to drop into the jar to help build the structure that stood before her now. Much like the little girl in Awana who had adopted her as a missionary. A tear threatened to squeeze out of her eye and fall, but at the sight of the young pastor walking across the road Karen blinked it away. "I--I remember," she said falteringly.

"Here comes Tony, the pastor, now," Lois said.

A young, brawny, dark-haired man like no one Karen had ever seen in Venezuela was walking toward them. "That's--the pastor?" Karen whispered. "He doesn't look very Venezuelan. And he can't be a day older than I am!"

Lois laughed. "That's what everyone says. He's Italian, and he's probably *not* any older than you. Maybe even younger!"

By then the young pastor had reached them, and Lois greeted him warmly. She introduced him to Karen, who shook his hand and said, "*Mucho gusto.*"

As Lois and the young man conversed in Spanish, Karen could tell by Lois's references to her that she was explaining to Tony about Karen's Seattle church. Karen excused herself and headed for the car to retrieve her cell phone. Tony understood and motioned for her to follow. Once inside the church, he gave them both a quick tour of the building. The clean, sturdy structure seemed out of place among the dilapidated houses surrounding it. Karen was impressed as she viewed the large open room, the carefully constructed wooden benches, the large cross hanging from the ceiling just off the platform. She had never before actually seen what her missions money had been used for. Karen remembered as a child badgering her parents for loose change and had even given the money in her piggy bank she'd been saving for a new bicycle.

Her eyes watered, and to cover a moment of embarrassment, she insisted that Tony stand up on the platform for a picture. She was careful to take a shot of each view of the building, including the cross and the front door which bore the words "*Iglesia Cristiana.*"

Now she would really have something to write home about!

When break ended and the missionaries had gone their separate ways, Karen was busier than ever. The new semester brought a new teacher and his family, which meant more food to prepare at each meal. Exercise class was two evenings a week if she chose to attend, and Karen was grateful for the physical outlet.

At least she had an electric typewriter for answering letters. Paul Birch had seen to it that one was delivered to her room the day Karen had asked. The dutiful correspondence was no longer a dreaded chore; she began to look forward to sharing her days with the people at home. Mr. Birch had told her to keep the typewriter as long as she needed, and Karen could see that she would be needing it for a long time! Within weeks after Christmas, she received nearly thirty cards and letters from supporters and friends, some mailed over a month before. Frustrated that the postal system took so much longer there, Karen was determined to personally answer each letter as soon as possible.

Spanish class was the first one after lunch, and Karen had to hurry with cleanup to be on time. But Lois had been right. With her current vocabulary, learning past-, present-, and future-tense greatly accelerated her ability to converse in Spanish.

Karen first experimented on the maids. To her surprise and delight, they understood her, and she understood what they said back to her when they spoke slowly. Lucy was a big help and began teaching Karen more and more names for items.

The maids were delighted when Karen showed them the kitten one afternoon. "*Como se llama?*" Rosalba asked.

"His name is Punkin," Karen explained.

"Punkin?" They looked puzzled.

Rob came along just then and tried to explain the kitten's name, saying that its fur was the color of pumpkins. "*Auyama*," he told them. "Pumpkin."

"*Auyama*," they giggled. "*Auyama.*"

"Well, Punkin sounds better," Karen said, but she had to admit it was funny, and giggled along with them. On impulse she said, "*Venga*" and indicated that they go with her. Inside her apartment, the maids followed while Karen led the way to her little bathroom.

"See?" she said, showing them a brown cardboard box with a half-moon penned on one side. The words read "*GATICO BAÑITO*". "Little kitty little bathroom" seemed fitting words for Punkin's litter box.

The maids pointed and snickered, while Punkin decided to wiggle out of Karen's arms and use the box, regardless of his audience. The women were still laughing as they walked back into the kitchen.

Bible club began again the following Saturday, and with each visit Pedro's mother would greet them pleasantly, her face alive with hope. Pedro was his usual animated self, playing and screeching, and waving his arms when he wanted something. As Karen watched him, she couldn't help but hope for a miracle.

The second week of February arrived, and Roxie and Karen drove up the hillside to pick up Pedro and his mother for the hospital visit Roxie had arranged. Carmelina wore a simple cotton dress, one that Karen had purchased for her at the school's rummage sale. She had brushed her long dark hair until it shone, hope gleaming in her eyes. Pedro, in clean shorts and shirt, looked ready for an adventure. The three women sang lively Bible songs in Spanish as they drove, Pedro clapping his hands along with them.

The large busy hospital was intimidating to Karen. She had no idea where to go or whom to ask, so she relied on Roxie, who had been there before and also spoke fluent Spanish. Their doctor was on the third floor, Roxie explained, and as the elevator door closed upon them Carmelina's eyes widened and she shot out one hand to steady herself. The car stopped at the third floor, and they piled out into the hall.

Pedro shrieked as they entered the doctor's reception area. In the center of the room on a small table were colorful blocks to match with the right holes in a larger block. There was also a coloring book and crayons and a few small cars. He gave Karen a big smile, which she returned. Oh, if only this doctor could help the little guy!

Karen tried to be patient. She prayed as she waited, and Roxie reached over and squeezed her hand. They all wanted Pedro to be well, but there were no guarantees.

The nurse called Roxie's name, and the three women stood. Since Karen's Spanish was limited, she suggested that Roxie go with the others, and she would wait.

It was the longest wait of her life.

When the door at last opened and they called Karen in, Roxie's face was grim, and it was obvious that Pedro's mother had been crying. With the doctor still present, Roxie explained that Pedro's hearing loss was inoperable.

"But what about a hearing aid?" Karen probed.

"We talked about that. They are *very* expensive, and even if we were to pay for it, minimal upkeep would be more than they could afford. But it isn't just that, Karen--" Roxie said softly. "A hearing aid would help him very little."

Karen fought back tears. She had so hoped for more than this.

The solemn group thanked the doctor, then left the office and walked slowly back down the hall. Pedro was as happy as ever, especially since the doctor had given him a piece of candy. They took the elevator back downstairs, walked through the lobby and outside the big glass doors into the early afternoon drizzle.

Just outside the double glass doors, Karen noticed a man, around thirty years of age, selling pencils. A crudely printed cardboard placard was placed nearby.

"What does it say?" Karen asked, trying to interpret the Spanish words.

Roxie hesitated. "It says: 'I'm deaf, please buy my pencils,'" she answered quietly. Karen was stunned. Would selling pencils on the street be Pedro's future if something wasn't done for him? Tears threatened to fall, but for Carmelina's sake she pasted on a bright smile and tried to be cheerful. The drive back to Rubio and up the mountain was a long, silent one, very different from their earlier commute.

Back at the school, though, Karen found it hard to stay melancholy for long. The students were buzzing with excitement. Valentine's Day was the next day, and the following Friday was the student union banquet. Young love seemed in full bloom. Girls whispered to each other the names of who had asked them to the banquet. Couples began pairing off, and it soon became obvious who had invited whom. Senior high students were selling carnations, two dollars each, with a typed message of one's choice attached. The grade school children baked and decorated large heart-shaped sugar cookies which they sold at a makeshift stand after supper each evening.

On Valentine's Day after school was out, the students set about delivering the flowers and messages. Karen was pleasantly surprised to receive six red carnations, all from different people! A high school student handed them to her as she was frying ham bits in bacon grease for baked potato bar that evening.

"Well, well," she said, pleased. Three were from grade school children, thanking her for the good meals.

"And especially red Jello", said one. Karen giggled at that comment. Having grown up with church potlucks where there was always some kind of gelatin salad in a mold, she no longer had a taste for the stuff. But the younger girls especially gobbled it up every time. Karen's heart warmed. She felt bad that she had been so wrapped up in her own--or, Pedro's--problems that she had completely forgotten about Valentine's Day. She didn't suppose it mattered. There was no one to do something special for. In the States she would have cooked a special meal for Jeff and probably sent valentines to some of her friends. But here, alone, it didn't seem to matter much. And it was far too expensive to send Valentine cards to the States, especially with no guarantee of how long the postal service would take!

Glancing at the fourth message, she saw that it was from Roxie, for being her friend. The fifth was from Paul and Lois Birch and the children, as a thank-you for all of her hard work.

Just then Rob breezed in, smiling from head to toe. "Hey, hey, ladies," he greeted, and, walking over to the two maids, handed them each a red carnation. "Happy Valentine's Day!"

Rosalba, obviously pleased, told him "*muchas gracias*" and after a quick sniff of its aroma went to put the flower in water. Lucy shyly took her carnation from his hand and thanked him as well.

"Wow, I can see you made quite a haul." Rob was directing the comment to her.

"Yes, they're from the children," she told him proudly. "I'm sure they were meant for you, too, since they're a 'thank-you' for all of our work and good food. Except this one--it's from Roxie. And one from Paul and Lois and their kids."

Rob pointed to the last red carnation in Karen's hand, which Karen had almost forgotten to read. "And--that one?"

"Oh! I almost forgot!" She silently read the attached card. *To a great partner. Happy Valentine's Day--Rob.*

Karen was touched. "Rob, that's sweet," she replied, a little embarrassed. "Thank you." With a quick wink he was gone, and Karen was left to wonder if the flower was a polite gesture or something more.

The following day the expected letter from Karen's office manager finally arrived. Karen lay sprawled on her bed and started to read. Punkin curled up beside her and began to purr softly, and Karen stroked his soft fur.

Charlene began with apologies for not writing sooner, but with work *and* home life so busy she hadn't taken the time. Nor, she explained, had she known what to write, since Karen's job was in limbo with all of the changes. The office structure was now about to change one more time. Charlene would soon be moving to Tacoma--would Karen be interested in the office manager position?

Karen's mouth dropped open as she continued.

...It would mean more money, and different responsibility than you had before. And of course you would inherit my office! Please understand, Karen, we're not just trying to fit you in--we feel that you would do an excellent job at this, especially since you have always made an effort to get along with everyone. The lawyers are recommending you for the position. You understand all of the policies and procedures better than anyone since you've been here the longest.

Please write me soon, or call with an answer. We'll be moving as soon as our house sells, probably early summer since that's the best time for the real estate market.

Karen let out an unladylike yelp. This was a dream come true! She had entertained ideas of managing the office, for the very reasons Charlene had mentioned. And to think she had to come to a foreign country to attain a promotion in the States!

She read the letter again to prove to herself it was real. Office manager. She had to go tell Rob!

With her hand on the doorknob, she caught herself. Would Rob even be excited for her? Obviously, she couldn't be in both places, and he had come to rely on her more and more all the time. She was his *partner*. He liked her. He depended on her. He kept reminding her that she was "only" here for a year.

Thinking better of it, she decided to say nothing to Rob about the news. After all, she'd never even told him about the first letter. She would tell her mother! Opening the desk drawer, she pulled out a piece of paper and began to write.

No sooner had she picked up her pen than someone began knocking at the door.

"*Señorita Karen*," a voice called out.

She opened the front door to find Rosalba beckoning her back to the kitchen. "*Venga, venga.*" She trailed behind while Rosalba led the way to the kitchen. Karen was surprised to find two men carrying boxloads of freshly butchered chickens and setting them on the kitchen counter.

"What's all this?" Karen asked.

"*Señor Rob?*" asked the older of the two, apparently a farmer, dressed in a dirty white shirt and dark cotton pants.

"He--he's not here," she tried to explain. "What are these for?" She tried to communicate with them in her limited Spanish as questions filled her mind. Had Rob ordered these, or were the men just trying to make a quick sale? Should she tell them to leave the chickens, or to take them away?

Bewildered, she turned to Rosalba with a questioning look on her face.

"*Está bien*," said Rosalba, nodding, indicating that this was standard practice. Karen shrugged and wondered why, then, had they come to get her? One man shoved a pen and a piece of paper under her nose, indicating that she sign it. As best as she could she deciphered the words on the receipt. She vaguely recalled Mr. Birch telling her that chickens were delivered from a nearby farm, so she supposed it was okay. Since she was signing for the chickens, however, she supposed she ought to count them. The paper said "100".

"*Un momento*," she told the farmer, setting down the pen. Walking over to the many boxes of fresh chickens, she began to count. But what she saw made her gasp in horror.

The room was silent and all eyes were on Karen.

"The feet!" she exclaimed. "They still have their feet on!" Puzzled, Rosalba walked over and tried to understand. Karen pointed to the large claws at the end of each wrinkled leg. "*Pies!*" she attempted in Spanish. "*Los pies!*" Rosalba nodded, and Karen gathered from her words that they were wonderful for making soup and that *Señor Rob* let them take the feet home. Thank goodness!

While Karen personally couldn't think of anything more disgusting, she tried to hide her distaste and went on counting. There were, as noted, one hundred chickens, all with feet still intact. Her stomach did a little lurch as she wondered if the heads, too, were still connected. Fishhead soup was a specialty in Venezuela, but she didn't know about chicken heads. Cautiously she turned one over, but to her great relief the heads were gone.

She let out a deep sigh and signed the paper, saying "*Gracias*" as graciously as she could muster. The men then walked out of the kitchen and out of the building, leaving Karen and the maids with two hundred ugly claws sticking straight up in the air.

Rob chose that moment to saunter in, carrying two large, netted sacks of oranges. "Oh, good, the chickens are here."

"Yes, and I hope you ordered them, because I just signed for them," she told him slowly, deciding not to mention the other matter for fear of him thinking her squeamish. Rosalba and Lucy's eyes were gleaming, though, and Karen knew she'd been had. In rapid Spanish, eyes twinkling, Rosalba told Rob what had transpired.

Rob, amused, watched Karen from the corner of one eye. Without a word he began to carry the boxes, one by one, into the large refrigerator. "Oh, by the way, Karen," he began when his back was turned, "I hope you don't mind--I added chicken's feet soup to next week's menu!"

Soon they were all laughing so hard their sides hurt.

* * *

Karen finished getting dressed, gave the kitten a quick hug, and locked her apartment. She ran up the stairs two at a time, almost knocking over Joe, who was on his way down.

"Whoa!" He flashed Karen a broad grin. "*No running on the stairs, girls!*" he ordered in his best dorm father's voice. "Going to a fire, are we?"

Karen laughed. "Just about as exciting! Roxie offered to take me to San C to shop!"

Joe gave a hearty laugh. "I know. Roxie feels it's her personal responsibility to show all new women missionaries the best places to spend their money. She's ready and waiting."

"What better to do on a rainy day?" Karen replied, laughing.

After spending the day running from one shop to another in San Cristobal, Karen was certain that Roxie *did* know the best places to shop. Karen's favorite was the outdoor mall, where several steps led down into a large open area featuring outdoor cubicles, almost like a sidewalk sale or booths at a fair. The *zapateria* in the main part of the city carried hundreds of pairs of shoes of all colors and designs, and Karen was pleased to find very Venezuelan dress shoes--bright orange with a colorful parrot down each side. "For a souvenir, if nothing else," she told Roxie with a grin on her face. "The price is certainly right!" In the outdoor mall she bought a lavender and black pants outfit, also traditional Venezuelan style, with the pants cut halfway up the leg. At a larger inside mall, clothing stores offered tiny cups of free coffee to shoppers. Karen spent many happy hours browsing through racks and racks of expensive dresses but purchased nothing.

Tired but happy, the women stopped in at the *panaderia* for a cup of *café con leche* before heading home. The rain came in a steady stream outside the little shop, and Karen was grateful to be warm and inside.

As the conversation turned to their upcoming Bible club on Saturday, Karen's thoughts turned to Pedro. "Roxie, I've just got to help him before I leave in June," she confided to her friend. "Aren't there any schools that will take him? Since his deafness can't be helped by surgery, there must be something else we can do."

"I don't know." Roxie slowly shook her head. "Would you like me to help you look?"

"I'd be very grateful. The right school could affect his whole future." Karen's eyes filled with tears.

Roxie assured her that she would do what she could. "For now, we'd better go!" she told Karen, noting that the rain wasn't letting up. Running to the car, they snapped their seatbelts tight and headed for the main road.

Without warning, the rain that had drizzled all day suddenly began to pour. Within half an hour, the streets were filled with water. Roxie, a deep frown furrowing her forehead, seemed deep in thought.

"Is anything wrong?" asked Karen.

"Not to worry you, but sometimes the road back to Rubio can be pretty hazardous in bad weather. I'm wondering if we should find a motel and wait it out, overnight if need be.

"I really feel like we need to get back, though," she went on. "The rain could get worse just as quickly as stopping, and then we could be stuck here for days! Oh well, here goes nothing." Claiming to know a better route for part of the way, Roxie drove up and around until they were practically overlooking the city. Other cars had the same idea, for within minutes a long line of cars followed them. Darkness had fallen by then, and the rain continued to pour. Roxie kept her eyes fixed on the headlights ahead of her, until they came to an abrupt stop.

"Uh oh."

"What's the matter?" Karen asked.

"I'm not sure. Wait here while I find out." Roxie grabbed her umbrella and left the car, returning moments later. "The road's washed out. We have to go back."

"Back?"

"The same way we came. There's another route to Rubio, but it's longer, and I was hoping we wouldn't have to take it. Should be safe enough, though."

As word spread, cars began turning around and going back down the winding hill. Roxie waited several times while drivers ahead of her stopped in an attempt to warn the cars still coming their way.

After what seemed an eternity, Karen noted that no one was following them. Behind them was darkness and ahead of them was a dark, winding road. Water gathered at the edges, but so far the way was clear.

"Have you taken this route before?" Karen asked.

"Uh huh. But not to save time, that's for sure! It's almost twice as long." She glanced at the illuminated clock shining out from the car's darkness. "Joe's going to be worried."

"Can't you call him?"

"There's no cell service in this area," Roxie told her. "Because the roads are so bad, we generally avoid being in San C after dark and it hasn't been a problem. But this could be."

Karen frowned.

"And it's not like the States where there's a rest stop or fast-food place you can duck into and wait out the storm. I think we're better to keep going." Karen could sense Roxie frowning in the darkness. "I should have thought ahead. I hope Joe doesn't worry, but I know he will. When I don't call, he'll probably figure it out. I just hope he doesn't start out after us."

They were silent most of the rest of the way home. Fortunately, though the water fell in torrents, the road was uninhibited. Within two hours, they had pulled into the back side of Rubio and within minutes could see the lights of the school.

Karen let out a loud sigh, then laughed. "I guess I didn't realize how scared I was!"

The tenseness in Roxie's face relaxed. "Yeah, me too, in a way. I didn't like the thought of getting stranded! But we're fine now. We'll be home in a jiffy."

"Thanks for taking me shopping," Karen said sincerely. "It was fun!"

"I'm glad you liked it, and I'm very glad I didn't go alone! I'd be a lot more nervous if you weren't with me, Karen!" Roxie gave her a bright smile.

They had pulled into the school's parking lot and Karen noticed Joe peeking out between the curtains on the second floor. "There's Joe!" she told Roxie. Karen thought distractedly how nice it would be to have someone to worry about her and wondered if Rob had given a second thought to her long absence.

Once inside the dorm, she had intended to follow Roxie upstairs but noticed lights on in the school's kitchen. "Roxie, thanks again," Karen told her friend, shaking the rain out of her long hair. "In spite of everything, I'm glad we went. It was truly an adventure!"

Roxie laughed and headed up the stairs. Just then Rob came out from the pantry. "Oh--hi!"

Karen, feeling much like a drowned rat, stopped in her tracks. "Hi yourself. What are you doing here this late? It's almost ten o'clock!"

"Checking on breakfast plans," he replied, as though it were the most natural thing in the world.

Karen knew good and well that once Rob left the kitchen after supper, he didn't set foot inside those doors again until morning. Breakfast plans were always laid out by the two of them even before supper was prepared. Pleased that he had come back to check on her, she hid a smug grin and asked, "Got any coffee?"

"Joe said you guys went to San C," Rob said moments later after fixing them each a cup of coffee with milk and sugar. "Did you have any trouble getting home?"

Karen began to relate the story to him, grateful that she did, after all, have someone to worry about her.

CHAPTER NINE

Spring Break: A Trip to the Mountains

The school quarter was passing quickly. With break coming up, Karen was trying to figure out what to do with all of her spare time. Over Christmas vacation, there hadn't been an opportunity to travel any distance because of the conference and holiday activities. But Spring Break was longer than a week. Almost all of the children would go home, and those who didn't would stay with staff families. The kitchen would be officially closed for ten days.

"What are you doing for Spring Break?" she asked Rob one afternoon as they put the finishing touches on supper preparations. "What do most people do?"

"Funny you should ask." He grinned. "I was just going to talk to you about it. The last day of break, I'd like to meet with you and go over planning for the next quarter. Or we can do that now if you want. But I was wondering.... would you be interested in going on a trip with some of us?"

Karen smiled, thoughtful. "Who all is going?"

"I don't know yet. Last year all of the singles went. Roxie and Joe can probably go, too, since all of their dorm kids go home. Hopefully Pete and Amanda, and me. Maybe a couple of others."

Karen's eyes lit up. "Sounds like fun! But where would we go?"

"Well, there's a town called Mérida about six hours from here. It's one of the highest points in Venezuela. From there you can ride a cable car to the top of the mountain, which is even higher--around 16,000 feet. There's snow up there usually, but even if there isn't, it's well worth the ride for the view alone. Last year we rode the cable car and just toured around. The women say it's the best shopping anywhere in Venezuela, though I wouldn't know about that!" He grinned. "Seriously, if you're not coming back next year, it *is* a great place to buy souvenirs, and gifts for your family. In Mérida, they sell almost everything that's handmade in Venezuela. Wall hangings, baskets, handmade dolls, wooden carvings--you name it."

"Sounds wonderful. Would we stay in a motel?"

Rob told her all about the motel the group had stayed in the year before, but said he hoped to change this year. "Someone told me of a little place I'd like to try--said it's really 'cultural'. And don't worry about expense. I think you'll find that a motel here costs about half what it would in the States, and you'll probably room with a couple of the other women. Since

Venezuela's economy is so bad, it's great for tourists. We'll all pitch in for gas--Joe will probably drive the school van--and buy our own food. What do you think?"

"I think it sounds wonderful" Karen exclaimed. "I'll talk to Roxie about it tomorrow!"

Roxie was delighted to learn that Karen was going. The two put their heads together and decided what to take and made a list of things to buy beforehand. Karen made certain she had bottled water for the trip and a packet of tissues. She remembered Roxie's words of warning, "The bathrooms along the road are NOT like the United States!" She carefully carried her passport in a hidden pocket under her shirt and put her Venezuelan money in a safe place. Karen was a little nervous at carrying so much cash. It would have been much simpler to pay with credit cards, but as Rob had explained, it wasn't that simple. Most stores required cash, and would not even accept a check, *especially* on an out-of-country bank!

The trip began the day after school was out. Paul and Lois had agreed to watch the kitten for her, and their children were thrilled. For the present, Karen had no responsibilities and not a care in the world.

Besides the individuals Rob had mentioned, also going on the trip were Cathy and Jennifer, Kelly--with whom Karen held no ill feelings by now, since Rob had shown her no special interest--and Kelly's grandmother. The older woman was somewhat of an icon at the school, since she had been dorm mother for twenty-eight years running. Now retired, and widowed, she lived near the school and helped out by repairing aprons and curtains and arranging housing for visiting parents. The woman, affectionately called simply "Grandma" by everyone since she was the school's oldest resident, was as young at heart as the day she had moved to South America, and the group was happy to have her along.

Packed and ready, the ten of them piled into the van. Joe drove while Roxie watched for good places to stop as well as ruts in the road. "I've wrecked a good tire or two in this country!" Joe explained. Grandma was eager with anticipation and took in all the sights and adventures as excited as a younger person might have. Pete and Amanda, recently engaged, held the look of wonder in their eyes. "I had to come all the way to South America to find him!" Amanda unabashedly told Karen. Pete just grinned.

Karen kept telling herself that she did *not* come all the way to South America to find her man. With that in mind, she tried not to isolate herself with Rob, since when the year was over, she would be going back to Seattle for good. Nevertheless, he seemed forever by her side. When first leaving Rubio, she had managed to squeeze in the middle seat with Kelly and Grandma. But upon returning to the van after a quick stop at the first rest area, she found the only available spot to be next to Rob. He gave her a warm smile as she edged in beside him.

Not that she was complaining. She and Rob had a companionable friendship and found themselves laughing together even when the rest of the group wasn't. Roxie kept giving Karen knowing looks, but Karen would pretend to frown at her.

When they arrived at the motel, Rob ran in to find out where to park, then returned with directions to the lot. After parking, they grabbed their bags and paraded down the street and into the little motel.

"So, this is the 'cultural' one, huh?" Karen asked him.

"That's what they say."

"Oh, I see what you mean," breathed Karen, at once impressed by brightly painted shuttered windows that opened onto the hall. With their windows open, they could all talk to each other! But she had a feeling that wasn't what Rob's friend had meant.

When they had all checked in, Karen found herself sharing a room with Amanda. The room was simple, containing a double bed and nightstand, a desk and chair, and a wooden rack for hanging clothes. On the nightstand was a lamp and a pitcher of cold water.

"Nice touch," mused Karen, indicating the pitcher of water.

"Yeah, just don't try drinking it!" warned Amanda, walking into the adjoining bathroom. "Uh-oh, no towels. I'll go ask for some."

"It *is* a little rustic," Karen admitted. "But the price is right. I wonder what the other rooms look like."

Grateful for the opportunity to get to know each other better, the girls stayed up late the first night talking. Amanda had grown up on a farm in a small town in Illinois, about as different from Karen as was possible. Strangely enough, though, she, too, had broken up with a man back home shortly before coming to Venezuela. "He just didn't understand," Amanda said sadly. "But no man is worth putting ahead of God. I know now why God wanted me here."

Karen stared at her. Was that why God had wanted her here, too? So she wouldn't marry the wrong man? She realized now that marrying Jeff would have been a tragic mistake. Since dating him her senior year in college, she more or less expected to marry him eventually. Everyone did. But he'd never had the zeal she so admired in other Christian men. And when he asked her to stay in the States for *him*, she should have realized that request as the ultimate selfishness.

The group soon realized why Rob's friend had called the motel *cultural*. Early in the morning a rooster crowing nearby in a neighbor's yard woke them all up. A parrot on the other side of the street, fascinated with the crowing, mimicked the rooster. Consequently, no one could sleep. After a cold shower (the manager later explained there was only hot water for one or two showers at a time!) Karen and Amanda met the others in the lobby. When they walked into the motel restaurant for breakfast, the waiter came out and apologized. The cook had shown up drunk, he explained, and had been sent home--but if they wanted coffee or pastries he could accommodate them. There was also some fresh fruit in the fridge. Keeping the circumstances in the spirit of adventure, the group had coffee and pastries, then went to freshen up before leaving for the day.

Karen heard a shriek from the bathroom and went running.

"Look!" Amanda pointed. "It's a lizard!" She had gone in to brush her teeth and noticed a green spot in the shower. By the time Karen had run breathlessly through the door, the lizard was slithering back down the drain.

The girls looked at each other and giggled. "Very cultural, indeed. Whatever happened to good ol' Holiday Inn?"

"Oh, that would have been boring!"

Leaving the motel behind, the group set out exploring on foot. Mérida was all that Rob had promised. Karen was grateful she had brought a lot of cash, as she found gifts for everyone at home as well as a few trinkets for herself. The many shops held key chains, wooden carvings, leather goods, ceramic figurines, clay pots, feather dusters, wall hangings, baskets, and more. And all at a reasonable price, she was pleased to discover. The others quickly explained, though, that she should try to get the items for less.

"But why? They're not too expensive."

"That's just the way it's done here. It's called 'bartering'," Joe explained.

Karen, though reluctant, decided to give it a try. "*No, gracias*," she said at the next shop after asking the price and started to walk away. The storekeeper quickly called her back with a better offer. She left the shop pleased but a little embarrassed.

"It seems like we're cheating them," she protested.

"Oh, not at all," Rob said. "They make the stuff for practically nothing." As the day wore on, Karen was enjoying setting her own sale price, as well as watching the others do the same.

After dropping off their packages at the motel and walking across the street for a quick lunch, the group piled into the van once again. Upon arriving at the *teleférico*, Joe parked while the rest of them hurried to get a place in line. Before going up, though, Rob insisted they buy some inexpensive snow gear in the shop at the bottom of the mountain. "At least mittens and snow caps," he advised. "Trust me, you'll be glad you did." Roxie, having been there before as well, agreed wholeheartedly.

The cable car ride was a memorable experience. Karen, a little afraid of heights, held her breath at first and was nervous about peering over the side. She felt a little dizzy and was unsure whether it was from her fear of heights or Rob's nearness beside her.

"Nervous?" she heard Rob ask.

"A little," she admitted. "I've been up in the Space Needle but it's not quite the same thing! And it wasn't hanging from just a few cables!"

The next thing she knew, Rob was holding her hand tightly. "If you get scared, squeeze," he said, leaning so close she could smell his aftershave lotion. "The way I look at it, if I trust an airplane, I should trust this thing! We're in God's hands both places!"

And my hand's in yours, Karen was thinking as she looked into in his caring brown eyes, at once oblivious to the rest of the group. She saw only Rob, a wool cap pulled down over his dark hair, and somehow knew that to be here, with him, was the safest place on earth. Squeezing his hand, she smiled back, then dared to look around her at the beauty. Below them, the valley rose and fell, and off to the right a river snaked its way along the canyon. The little town of Mérida lay miles below. Far off in the distance a mountain range loomed.

"Wow," she breathed. "It looks just like the pictures of the Andes Mountains we used to see in grade school."

"Karen," laughed Pete, ever the teacher, "those *are* the Andes Mountains!"

The group shared a good laugh, and Karen laughed at herself. "I never was good in geography," she admitted.

The cable car stopped at three stations along the way. At each one, the entire group, which included about fifteen strangers, left the car to walk around. One station featured a large gift shop, while another contained virtually nothing but an oversized statue of a famous South American leader. Karen asked Roxie to snap a picture of her with the imposing figure, which gave Rob ideas of his own.

"Take one of me and Karen," he urged.

"Karen and *me*," Karen corrected with a droll look on her face.

"Yeah, but you *are* Karen," Rob teased back. "Why would you need a picture of you AND yourself?"

Laughing, Karen hit him on the arm with one loose mitten, just as Roxie snapped the photo. "Hey, wait!" Karen protested. "I wasn't ready!" Roxie took a quick second shot as Rob snuggled close and placed an arm around Karen's shoulders, then it was time to go. As the cable car moved further up the mountain, Karen snapped many more photographs of the breathtaking scenery all around her, and several of her group of friends.

When they had finally reached the top, Karen gave a shriek of delight. Even before disembarking, she could see that snow covered the ground. She had felt silly buying a snow cap and mittens in sunny South America, but now her teeth clattered, and she shivered. "It's just like home!" she exclaimed. Though no longer on the cable car, Rob kept a tight hold on her hand, releasing it only when Amanda aimed a snowball directly at him. Karen's chest was heavy as she tromped through the snow. Joe had warned them to walk slowly at the top, since at that elevation it could be difficult to breathe. After they were all worn out from frolicking, they walked back inside the station to browse in the little gift shop and enjoy a cup of hot chocolate before taking the car back down.

Rob again sat next to Karen and took her hand. Roxie brushed past Karen on her way into the cable car. "You're beginning to have that look in your eye," Roxie whispered.

"What look?"

"You know--like Amanda." Roxie winked and sat down.

Karen, stunned, was suddenly without words.

Excited but tired, the group was quiet as the cable car made its way back down. A light rain had begun to fall, and by the time they reached the end of their ride, rain was coming down steadily. The group bolted out of the *teleférico* and made a run for the van.

After driving across town and entering the motel, Karen immediately noticed that water was *inside* their building as well as outside. Remembering the home of the seamstress in Rubio she had visited, whose house had an open courtyard, she wondered if this building were the same. But to the group's amusement, they discovered that there was a large leak near Joe and Roxie's room, and several smaller ones nearby. The hotel manager had placed numerous plastic containers in the hallway to catch the dripping.

"Cultural?" Kelly remarked, glancing over at Rob. He merely grinned.

"What's on the agenda for tomorrow?" Amanda asked an hour and a half later when they were seated at a nearby Chinese restaurant waiting for their order.

"Oh, Joe, we've got to show Karen the Beethoven clock," suggested Roxie.

"The Beethoven clock?"

"Oh, yes, I remember," put in Grandma. It's a large clock across town, and every hour on the hour the chimes play a different Beethoven song! I've never stayed around long enough to listen to all twelve, but I've heard five or six of them!"

"And what about the zoo?" asked Amanda, who had never been to Venezuela before either. "I've heard it's really nice, even better than the Seattle Zoo."

"Ah, if you've seen one zoo, you've pretty much seen 'em all," shrugged Rob, whose comment was met with scowls from several of the women. Seeing he was outnumbered, he relented. "But, on the other hand, I've never actually seen a South American gorilla, have you, Joe?"

They laughed at Rob's quick change of opinion. This time he was sitting directly across the table from Karen and between Pete and Grandma. As the waiter arrived and each savored their various meals, the group grew quieter as the evening wore on.

"What a day! Let's NOT set the alarms," Karen suggested. "Anybody disagree with that?"

"I don't think we'll need to," Rob reminded them. "I'll plan on seeing each of you in the hallway one hour after the rooster crows!"

Karen had originally planned to stay up late playing cards with the rest of the group but found herself too exhausted. The card players ended up being just the guys. The women excused themselves and retired to their rooms.

The second day was as enjoyable as the first. This time they ate breakfast at a restaurant near the zoo, which would be their second stop. After several hours of viewing animals, Karen was inclined to agree with Rob's earlier comment. The zoo was quality and would have been the envy of Seattle's Woodland Zoo. But she was tired of walking, the heat was giving her a headache, and the musty smell of the animals was beginning to make her feel nauseous. Not wanting to be the first to suggest they go, she said nothing of her feelings until they came to the end of the walkway and stopped on the little moss-covered bridge to take pictures of the waterfalls.

"Feels good to rest!" she said loudly. Grandma was looking a little worn out herself. "Have you had enough walking for one day?" Karen asked her. Karen *had* noticed Grandma pacing herself along the way.

"Most days I can keep up with you young people just fine," Grandma said after taking a deep breath. "But whenever you're ready to go, so am I."

They quickly reached a unanimous consent and piled into the van once again. After stopping for a hamburger, they drove across town to view the famous clock. The Victorian-looking clock, a muted green with yellow and tan embellishments, reminded Karen of the little town of Leavenworth, Washington, she had once visited.

Roxie noted with disappointment that the top of the hour had just passed, and they would have to wait another fifty-five minutes to hear the next song. Taking advantage of the wait, Karen asked a passerby to snap a picture of all of them in front of the clock, then Roxie gave the man her phone as well. After the group shots, Pete and Amanda decided to walk around the little park, and the others soon followed. Then, lounging in the cool grass, they talked and rested until the clock was ready to chime again. They could hear the clock's inner workings as it prepared to play, then a beautiful song began. Still lying on the grass, Karen closed her eyes and took in its beautiful melody. Soothing to the soul. Very relaxing. In fact, she could almost go to sleep....

"Karen, time to go!" Someone nudged her. Yawning, she realized with some embarrassment that she *had* nodded off. Laughing, she allowed Rob to pull her to her feet and keep hold of her hand once she was on firm footing.

"Anyone for pizza?" Pete asked.

"Oh, yeah," Rob was saying. "Remember that place we went last year where they have American music?"

"We just had lunch!" Jennifer reminded them.

"That's true," piped in Roxie. "Joe, let's take a nice long drive around the lake. Remember all of those beautiful homes?"

Rob managed to squeeze in next to her as they piled into the van. Karen was relieved that he made no attempt to touch her. She was finding it very difficult to keep her resolve with him always beside her. She would only be in for heartbreak if she gave in.

Karen was delighted with the pizza place. The old-fashioned jukebox played songs in English, and the group plugged in money for one tune after another. Other patrons were enjoying the American visitors, and the restaurant soon became rowdy with laughter.

That evening they all stayed up late playing a game of cards. Tomorrow they would have to drive back to Rubio, and no one seemed to want the evening to end.

Weeks later as Karen gazed at the photographs she had taken, she was glad she had so many pictures of the trip. Rob had shared with her the ones he'd snapped, and Karen wondered what he would do with the picture of him and her alone in the *teleférico* station. A good one of both of them, Karen considered having it enlarged and framed, but that would be admitting there was something between them. For now, it would just have to sit in her phone with the rest of the shots.

CHAPTER TEN

A Taste of South America

Karen's legs hurt. She stopped climbing and glanced up the hill in front of her. Most of the group was almost to the top. Wiping the perspiration from her brow, Karen wondered why she had ever let Roxie talk her into accompanying the junior girls on a hike up Mt. Baldie. The altitude was so much higher in South America that Karen's chest felt heavy and breathing became more difficult. The young girls, running and giggling, seemed oblivious to the effect of the warm mountain air.

"You doin' okay?" she heard Roxie's cheerful voice from behind.

"Whew! This makes me feel really out of shape!" Karen told her. "Although I haven't worked out lately, except for exercise class, I didn't think I was that bad!"

Roxie only laughed. "It's just the altitude. Don't push it any harder than you want to. Remember, I've been here for five years, so I'm used to it. And Joe's a natural born climber." Joe, already at the top, stood holding a walking stick and surveying the valley.

Karen took a sip from her water bottle as she slapped at a mosquito.

"You comin', Aunt Karen?" she heard one of the girls ask. The little voice was all it took to get her going again. Refreshed from the drink, she said, "You bet!" and started up the hill.

Karen wished Rob could have come, but he had other plans for their only day off. In the week since school had started again, Karen had not been alone with him at all except for working side by side with him daily. It was probably just as well that he hadn't come. Though still determined not to get involved with him, her emotions seemed to be spinning out of control ever since Spring Break. In truth, she had tried to avoid being alone with him. With only a few months to go, she would have to be careful not to go home with a broken heart.

Karen would have preferred a cooler day for the climb, but she had no idea when or if she would be asked to go again. And she was *determined* to climb Mt. Baldie at least once before the school year ended!

The group soon reached the top, and the descent went much faster than the initial climb. Though Roxie warned the girls not to run the whole way, most did, and the adults scrambled to keep up.

When the alarm went off the next morning, Karen ignored it. Her head was warm, and her eyes hurt too much to open. She groaned. Did this job come with sick days, she wondered?

Uncertain what to do, she crawled out of bed and groped her way into the living room, a little frightened. She could not remember burning her eyes over hot steam, but there was definitely something wrong. Through squinted eyes she reached for her phone and called Rob. No response. She sleepily called Roxie.

"Hello?" a sleepy voice answered.

"Joe--let me talk to Roxie." She waited to hear Roxie's voice, then said, "Rox, it's me, Karen. I feel really sick. Can you help Rob with breakfast?"

"Sure, I was just about to get the girls up. What's wrong?"

"My head feels warm, and my eyes hurt something awful. I just want to go back to bed! Rob doesn't answer his phone so he doesn't know. He'll be here in about half an hour."

"Sure, sweetie, I can help. I'll explain everything to Rob. Just leave your door unlocked, and I'll be over to see you after breakfast."

"Thanks. You're a dear." Karen hoped a couple hours of rest would do the trick. She flipped the lock on the door and made her way back into the bedroom. Exhausted, she dropped back onto the bed, too tired even to lift the covers.

From somewhere far away she heard a voice calling to her. "Karen? Karen?"

"What, Mom," she responded automatically, then realized it was Roxie, not her mother, who stood near her bed. Through slits in her eyes, she could see the concerned look on Roxie's face.

"Karen, how *are* you?"

A quick glance at the clock told Karen it was now two hours later. "Oh," she moaned. "My eyes. They must be sunburned or something. I guess yesterday's hike was too much for me. And my head...I'm so hot. Can you open a window?"

"Here, drink some water," Roxie ordered. "And get between the sheets."

Karen obeyed. The kitten, sleeping on the end of the bed, meowed at being disturbed.

"Do you have a thermometer?" Roxie asked, feeling Karen's forehead as Karen sipped the cool water Roxie had given her.

"Uh uh."

"Okay, stay put. I'll be right back."

"I'm not going anywhere," Karen attempted to joke. The next thing she was aware of was a cool cloth on her forehead. Thank God for Roxie. "You're back," she said out loud.

"No," replied a deep voice. "It's me. Rob."

Karen was too sick to be concerned for her appearance or to wonder what Rob was doing in her bedroom. "Oh, Rob--I'm sorry about breakfast. I'll be okay after I get more sleep. My eyes--there's gravel in them or something."

"Don't worry about the kitchen," he told her. "Just get well."

She longed to see his face but was not about to open her eyes again for anyone. "I'll be fine. You don't suppose it was one of your 'unbeatable burgers' do you? Those parasites or whatever they are?"

"No, I don't think so," he said softly. "It's not giardia. But Roxie seems to think you have all the symptoms of dengue fever."

"What--what's that?"

"Just that--a fever. It's very common in South America, usually carried by mosquitos. The symptoms are like yours--burning eyes, high fever--"

"Do I have a fever?"

"Yes. Don't you remember Roxie taking your temperature?"

"No. Just a few minutes ago?" Karen asked, not realizing that her friend had left the room hours earlier.

"No--*this morning*."

"This morning--but--what time is it?" She squinted in a vain attempt to see the clock.

"It's after two o'clock in the afternoon. Listen, Karen, you need to eat something. I'm going to bring you some cereal or a bowl of soup. Put something decent on so you can sit up in bed. Okay?" His voice took on a stern tone. Even in her feverish state Karen could tell he was concerned about her. She heard him opening a drawer. "Here--here's a T-shirt," he said, tossing something onto the bed.

"Okay, boss." Karen yawned and sat up as he left the room. She could hear his long strides as he walked through the living room, then she heard the closing of the front door. She sat up and looked around. Oh, she was so tired. And hot. The long night shirt she was wearing was perfectly modest as long as she stayed in bed, but Karen wrapped a robe around herself anyway and made her way to the bathroom, not knowing how soon Rob would return. The sudden movement did not go over well with her stomach, and she rushed to make it just in time to vomit over the side of the toilet.

Worn out, she stayed on the floor of the bathroom and leaned her head back against the wall. That was how Rob found her when he returned with the orange juice and cold cereal a few minutes later. He carried her back to bed, lifting the sheets and laying her tenderly between the covers. She was trying to go to sleep again when he shook her gently awake. "Karen, Karen--you really need to drink something. Otherwise, you'll dehydrate."

"Doctor's orders?" Karen asked groggily.

"Doctor's orders. Here, sit up and drink this." He offered her the glass of orange juice, which she drank gratefully.

"You make a good doctor," she said, feeling a little better. "Ever think of changing professions?"

"My bedside manner isn't too great when I'm worried about a patient," Rob said gruffly. "Now, I'm going to check on you every hour or so to make sure you're okay. And Roxie will be down during the night to take your temperature again."

Karen didn't understand. "Why, what's all the fuss? I just need some rest. Been working too hard...."

Rob's face was solemn. "You're very ill, Karen. We just want to make sure the fever runs its course with no complications."

Karen barely heard his words. All she wanted to do was close her eyes and go back to sleep. "Punkin," she suddenly remembered, hearing the kitten scratching in his litter box. "Make sure Punkin has food and water, okay?"

"Okay," Rob promised.

"What about the kitchen?" Karen asked sleepily. But she did not hear Rob's answer as she drifted off to sleep.

Karen remembered little of the next few days. She heard voices of people as they came and went. They talked to her, poked her, felt her forehead, took her temperature, and brought her food and water. Only barely aware of what was going on around her, she just wished they would all leave her alone and let her sleep.

She awoke one afternoon to find a lovely array of fresh flowers on her nightstand. Yawning, she sat up in bed, wondering who they were from. Curious, she picked up the handmade greeting cards that stood next to them. Roxie's girls had decorated a card for her, as did Amanda's first-grade class. "We miss your food," one had written. "Get well soon, Aunt Karen," wrote another.

Karen smiled. How sweet they were, and how she missed their chatter and smiles!

Still wondering about the flowers, she heard a tap at the door and a voice call out, "Karen, it's me, Roxie."

"Roxie, come talk to me. I'm beginning to feel human again."

Roxie entered the room, a plate of food in her hand and a bright smile on her face. "Boy, am I glad to hear that! We were a little worried about you for a while."

"Why?"

"Well, you--you don't remember anything?"

"Hmm, just that Rob brought me food and you took my temperature and then left, and--and people kept feeling my forehead. That's about all. I threw up once. I've been sleeping mostly. What day is it, anyway?"

"It's Saturday," Roxie replied, setting down the plate. "You got sick on Tuesday, which makes this the fifth day you've been lying here!"

Karen could scarcely believe it.

"You were delirious," Roxie explained. "Your fever was quite high. You were saying things that didn't make sense." She hesitated. "You even called me 'Mom' a time or two, and you seemed to think Rob was somebody named 'Jeff.'"

"Oh, no!" Karen's hands flew to her face. "Did I call him that to his face?"

"I don't think so. But you asked me if Jeff was coming back. The flowers are from him, by the way."

"From Rob?"

"Yes. Poor Rob. He was quite worried about you, too. He's been here as much as his schedule--and Paul Birch--would allow! Barb's been helping out in the kitchen so he could juggle classes and the kitchen workload. And taking care of you."

"Taking care of me?" she echoed.

"Yes. I was here some too, of course, and even Lois, but--Rob insisted on staying with you. I think he really cares for you, Karen."

Karen was touched. "But--but he hardly even knows me."

"He knows you better than anyone else does," Roxie said softly. "He works with you every day." She paused. "All last year he didn't give anybody a second look. I have a feeling your coming along has ruined all of his wonderful notions of permanent bachelorhood. I saw the way he looked at you in Mérida. Believe me, the man is sunk!" Roxie gave her a knowing smile.

Karen was too stunned to answer. Then, slowly, she said, "He--he's never really said anything--"

Roxie only smiled. "Well, believe me, he's said a lot by his actions the last few days." She stood up, ready to leave. "I'd better get back to the dorm. I'm SO glad you're better, Karen. Just rest for another day or so, okay? Barb's planning on working until you're back up and running, and Amanda's going to help with club today. Just rest and get well. All right?"

Karen rewarded her with a big smile. "Okay. And Roxie--thanks. For everything."

Punkin chose that moment to lie on her forehead, which was his custom. "Hi sweetie," she said softly. "Off you go, I've got to eat my dinner." Setting the kitten next to her, she sat up in bed. After eating the delicious meal Roxie had brought, Karen showered, then brushed her teeth and put on fresh make-up.

She didn't see Rob again until that evening, long after she knew the picnic was over and the leftovers put away. She didn't know whether to feel grateful or embarrassed, and in truth was a little of both. Rob had seen her in her most humble state. She *did* remember him helping her back to bed after she got sick in the toilet bowl that first night. How many guys would stick around in the rough times? Certainly not Jeff.

After freshening up she had changed into a pair of sweats and a flowered T-shirt and was feeling like an entirely different person. She stripped her bed of the dirty sheets and added fresh ones, then threw the bedspread back on and walked out to the living room. Suddenly exhausted again, she dropped onto the living room sofa and closed her eyes, only to hear a knock at the door. She got up slowly and opened it.

"Karen?" Rob blinked.

"You were expecting, maybe, Godzilla?"

The look on his face was one of great relief. "Karen, it's great to see you up and around."

"It's great to BE up and around. Come on in. I'm not contagious, am I? Although I guess you'd have it by now if you were going to get it."

He stood gawking at her as though he had never seen her before. "Uh--no, I won't get it. Are you--all better?" he asked, entering the room and seating himself on the sofa.

Karen perched on the edge of the chair. "Ninety percent. I'm still very tired. Roxie says I should just rest a couple more days, but are you doing okay without me?"

Rob looked as though he wanted to say something else, but responded, "Uh--yeah--I mean, Barb's helping out. We're doing fine. We--the kids miss you, of course--they've been asking about you." He was stumbling over his words. "But really, don't worry about a thing. Just concentrate on getting better."

Karen smiled. "I'll do that. Oh, and Rob--thank you for the flowers. They're lovely."

Rob grinned. "You're welcome."

"And--" Karen did not know what to say to him for being her "nursemaid." She was almost too embarrassed to mention it, but his loyalty should not go unnoticed or unappreciated. "Thanks for everything else you did. I mean, for taking care of me."

"No problem. You don't think I want to be in that kitchen alone the rest of the year, do you? I had to make sure my partner got well!"

She smiled.

"Do you feel up to a night out?"

"Uh, maybe in a few days. What did you have in mind?"

"Well...next Friday evening there's a special evangelistic meeting up in El Poblado. The church people at Cascarí would really like to go, but no one in their group drives, so I offered to take a few in my jeep. Would you like to go with me?"

Karen suppressed a chuckle. She had yet to go on a "real date" with Rob, but he seemed to enjoy her company as much as she enjoyed his. She should turn him down, but somehow after all he had done it would seem rude. And besides, they wouldn't actually be *alone* with a carload of people!

As if reading her thoughts, he continued. "It's not really like a date, just a church thing. I thought you might enjoy the cultural aspects."

"I'd love to," she said sincerely. "And Rob, I hate to ask, but--"

"Yes?"

She grinned mischievously. "I'm dying for a cup of coffee."

Rob grinned at her as he stood up and headed for the door. "Be right back."

Karen sighed and leaned back against the cushions. What more could a girl ask for?

The following Friday as soon as supper cleanup was done, Karen walked back to her apartment to get ready. She dressed with care in anticipation of the evening ahead. Rob had said he would come by in half an hour, which didn't give her much time. The little church was almost an hour's drive, so she had promised to be ready.

Punkin, wanting to help, climbed up on her shoulders to watch her refresh her make-up.

"You're getting almost too big for that, Punkin," she told him, astonished at how much the kitten had grown in the last four months.

When Rob knocked, Karen grabbed her purse and opened the door. "I'm ready," she told him, shutting off the light and closing the door behind her.

"I can see that," he replied, smiling broadly. "Who was it that said women always keep men waiting, anyway?"

"Probably my father," said Karen with a laugh. "About my mother!" Together they walked down the hall and out to his jeep. "Who all are we picking up?"

"I'm not really sure. I just promised I'd be there and if there isn't enough room someone will have to stay behind." He drove the jeep up the same steep roads Lois had taken weeks earlier. At night the road seemed even steeper and more treacherous. Karen sucked in her breath as they rounded a curve.

Rob only laughed. "Don't worry, you're in good hands. Les will get us there in one piece."

"Les?"

Rob patted the dashboard. "Les. The road LES traveled--usually the one no one else dares to take!"

Karen giggled at the reference to the famous Robert Frost poem. "Now *that's* appropriate." She sat back and tried to enjoy the scenery. The warm air caressed her hair as it blew through the open jeep windows. She let out a long, satisfied sigh. "It's so good to be outside after being cooped up for so long. And it's beautiful, isn't it? What's that flower over there?" she asked, pointing.

Rob began identifying the various greenery, and before Karen knew it, they had arrived at Cascarí. As they turned a corner and pulled up beside the little church, Karen was shocked to see that there was a whole crowd waiting for Rob to arrive. She glanced over at him, her eyes questioning. He only shrugged, and they both got out of the jeep.

Before Karen knew what was happening, the entire group of churchgoers had piled into the jeep. Several sat on each side of the jump seats in the very back, four in the middle seat, and one in the front. Beside Rob.

Beside Rob!

It took a minute for Karen to realize that the only place left to sit was on the floor in the very back, between the jump seats. She was grateful that she had worn her denim skirt and vest. After all, they were both comfortable and washable. She headed for the back door and climbed inside, settling herself among the others.

"Karen?" She looked up to see Rob standing just outside the back of the jeep, ready to close the door. A question was on his face.

"It's okay," she told him, grinning. "Really. Chalk it up to one more adventure!"

He gave her a warm smile. "If you're sure. Thanks, Karen." With a quick wink he closed the door and started the jeep, talking and joking with the men in the front. The women around her attempted to make conversation, and Karen was pleased that she could answer some of their questions.

By the time the jeep pulled up in front of the El Poblado church, Karen's legs were stiff, and her body was sore from sitting on the floor during the long, bumpy ride. She was relieved when the back door opened, and Rob offered a hand to help her out. They filed into the church and Karen was pleased that she could, at least, have a seat beside Rob on the hard wooden bench.

"These things don't really last two hours, do they?" Karen whispered to Rob, mostly in jest. She had heard stories of meetings like this. And two hours of a Spanish sermon would be a little more than she could take.

"Anything's possible," Rob told her with a grin.

After much lively singing, which Karen thoroughly enjoyed, the speaker began to preach. After a full hour, he was still going strong. A long sermon, by anyone's standards! Rob flashed her a knowing grin as Karen glanced at her watch. To Karen's surprise, she understood a little of the sermon, but was relieved when the speaker said a final prayer and sat down. It was already nine-thirty and, besides the hour-long drive back to school, they still had to drive to Cascarí to drop off the rest of the group.

A plate was passed as the offering was taken. Then to Karen's dismay, the lights were turned off and a film about Jesus was projected on the bare white wall on one side of the room.

Rob turned to grin at her. "What'd I tell ya?" After Karen returned his smile, Rob reached over and took her hand, holding it tightly during the entire film. The show was well-done, and Karen watched with interest, trying not to think about Rob's hand tightly holding hers or how fast her heart was beating. Though the words were not always ones she understood, Karen could easily depict what was happening as Jesus first chose his twelve disciples, then preached to the multitudes, then calmed the stormy sea. As Jesus was thrown back and forth between the leaders of the time, Karen found her eyes filling with tears. After Christ's death on the cross, and the women's visit to an empty tomb giving evidence of a risen Lord, the film ended. The large room was quiet except for the sound of weeping. When the invitation was given, several raised their hands to accept Christ.

Karen wiped the tears from her own eyes and let go of Rob's hand after giving it a squeeze. The group waited for one guest who had lingered behind to pray, then piled into the jeep once more and headed back to Cascarí. Karen again took her place between the jump seats. Pressing the light on her watch, she could see that it was well after ten o'clock. She yawned and leaned against the seats. She barely heard the animated conversation around her as the gentle rocking of the jeep rambling along the winding roads soon lulled her off to sleep. She awoke as they pulled into Cascarí, surprised that they had already arrived.

After the group disembarked, Karen went up front to sit beside Rob. The church people were very grateful for the ride, calling out their "Thank-you's" and "God bless you's." It warmed Karen's heart to see how such a small gesture of friendship was so appreciated. She returned their waves until the jeep was down the road and around a corner.

"Whew! That was quite an experience!"

Rob laughed. "That's for sure."

She glanced over at him sympathetically. "I'll bet you're tired. I'm sorry I can't offer to help you drive!"

"Want to?"

Karen laughed. She knew he was only kidding--she had no license to drive here, and it frightened her just to *ride* on these roads! "No way," she said firmly.

"By the way, how was Mt. Baldie?" Rob said suddenly. "I never got a chance to ask you about it."

"Oh, it was great! Beautiful scenery from the top. I could have lived with one less mosquito bite, though!"

"Yeah, the one that made you so sick," Rob said sympathetically.

"By the way, what did you do on your day off?"

"Did you see the guy who sat where you're sitting earlier? His name's Armando. His wife Maria was in the middle seat. Anyway, I helped him and his family move."

"Oh. Did you borrow a truck or something?"

Rob shook his head. "Would you believe, it only took three loads in the jeep to move their stuff! With all of the materialism in the States, and simply a different standard of living, it's quite a contrast to meet people like these. They're very poor, and yet they have all they need. Especially the Christians. They're so full of joy and, to all appearances, not lacking for anything."

Rob kept talking, and Karen found herself mesmerized listening to his words as the jeep gently rocked her to sleep once again. She quickly awoke as her head jerked forward.

Embarrassed, she glanced over at Rob. "Sorry. I guess I'm a little sleepy. I feel about as wobbly as a wet noodle."

"Your body's still recovering. Lean back," Rob suggested.

"But I was going to stay awake and talk to you," Karen protested.

"It's okay," Rob insisted. "Really. Just lean your head back and relax."

Karen could barely see him in the darkness. She sighed, too tired to argue and grateful for the suggestion. She soon fell asleep once again and was vaguely aware of the rumble of the jeep as it carried them along.

It was after midnight when they pulled up outside the dorm. Karen's head had somehow fallen onto Rob's shoulder, and she was enjoying the nearness of him. She gradually became aware that Rob was gently shaking her awake.

"Hey, Sleeping Beauty, we're here."

Karen yawned and lifted her head off of his shoulder. Rob was so close she could hear him breathing. Remembering her resolve not to get too involved with him, Karen sadly resisted a strong impulse to lean into his arms and let him hold her close. She sighed and pulled away.

Rob's eyes questioned, but he said nothing.

"It's late," Karen said quietly, leaning as far toward her side of the car as possible. "You don't need to walk me in. Morning's going to seem very early tomorrow!"

Rob looked at her admiringly. "You were a real sport tonight, Karen," he said. "Ya know that?"

She blushed. "Thanks. And thanks for asking me. It was quite an evening."

"Yes," Rob said quietly. "And you're quite a girl."

Karen could feel her resolve melting. Flashing him a longing glance, she climbed out of the jeep and walked slowly to the dorm.

CHAPTER ELEVEN
Help for Pedro

U h oh, we're almost out of pancake batter," said
Rob. The children were beginning to file in for
breakfast. He kept flipping pancakes on the
griddle and asked, "Karen, can you make
some? Maybe...half the recipe?"

"Uh--sure," she agreed, "is the recipe in the box on
the counter?" She quickly found it and began to follow
the directions. Although they were in Spanish, she had
memorized the simple baking ingredients for most
items: *harina* for flour, *azucar* for sugar. She began to
add the dry ingredients. After mixing in the baking
powder, she added the required water and handed the
bowl to Rob. "Will this be enough?"

"Sure--thanks," he said, pleased, and immediately
poured some onto the hot griddle. The pancake began to
bubble. "Wow, these are really light," he commented.
"Did you follow the recipe?"

"Uh huh," she murmured, pouring hot syrup into
serving bowls. The high school girls were busy pouring

milk into pitchers and carrying the pitchers to the tables. As the children walked by, Karen dished hot pancakes onto their plates as they smiled back at her. "Morning, Aunt Karen."

Rob was still muttering. "Karen, these are practically bubbling off the griddle! Wow!"

"Well, I just followed the recipe," she answered a little defensively, taking a plate over to him for more pancakes.

"How much baking powder did you put in?"

"Uh, whatever it said--I think it called for a cup--"

"A cup! No wonder!"

"Here, let me look." She walked over to the card file. "Yes, 'one C.'"

"Karen--'one C' isn't a cup, remember? 'C' stands for *cuchara*! It should be one tablespoon!"

"Oh no--" she looked stricken.

Rob was doubling over in laughter. "Don't worry, they're edible. But don't bother to come and get them, they may crawl there first!"

They shared a good laugh, and the children at the window giggled. Roxie walked by with her junior girls, and they joined in laughing as well. "That's like the time I was making cookies," Roxie admitted. "Since 'T' is for *tasa*, not tablespoon, and 'C' is for *cuchara*, not cup, I had put in only three tablespoons of flour when I was trying to figure out why so little!"

"At least too little is easily fixable!"

The next morning, she and Rob were to fix breakfast for 52 Venezuelan pastors who were using the school grounds for a conference. Since the children ate in their own dorms on Saturday morning, the dining hall was available and could be readied the night before. That Friday afternoon, she and Rob discussed the menu.

"Remember, Venezuelans like lots of coffee and hot milk," Rob advised. "Last year they kept coming into the kitchen and asking for it. Let's just put a pitcher of hot milk next to the coffee pot. It's a good thing the coffee bar is finished. Otherwise, they'd be in the kitchen ALL THE TIME!"

Karen grinned. Her idea for a coffee bar has inspired even more changes in the kitchen. Formica shelves replaced the old wooden ones which had badly shed sawdust on the clean dishes. Doug had painted all the freezer shelves bright white. Rob and Doug put their heads together and worked out the idea for a spice cupboard which, recently finished as well, now proudly displayed three shelves of spices at arm's length.

"And we'll have scrambled eggs with the cinnamon rolls," Rob went on. "Cinnamon rolls aren't a Venezuelan dish, so they're a treat for the men. And cut-up melon of several varieties."

"What about sausage?" Karen asked.

"Yes, if I can get it today. The meat market doesn't always have it. If they don't, we can slice up some ham. Maybe that would be better, anyway."

They were so deeply engrossed in conversation neither had noticed a man standing just inside the front door of the dining hall. Rob glanced up and walked over to talk to him. When he came back, he gathered up all of the kitchen's large knives while Karen watched, puzzled, while he disappeared again.

"Who's that?" Karen asked when he returned.

"A friend of Señor Mantilla, evidently. He needs work. I figure, our knives need sharpening anyway, and I'll pay him ten *bolivares* per knife. I offered him some food, too. I hope that was okay with you. He doesn't look like the type who'll hang around with his hand out."

Karen smiled. "Of course." She was again touched at Rob's thoughtfulness. He did not approve of slothfulness or begging, but when a Venezuelan offered to work for pay, Rob did his best to find them a job. She gazed over at him. Ever since Spring Break, it was becoming more and more difficult for Karen to work with him, knowing that in two short months they would separate. For good. He seemed to share her thoughts, and except for holding her hand at the recent church service had not approached her in a personal way.

As daylight streamed in the window the next morning, Karen was startled to realize that her alarm had not gone off. The usual bright numbers were not lit up, and her phone told her she had overslept for forty minutes. Frantic, she ran to the bathroom and splashed cold water on her face. Doing her make-up in record time, she ran a comb through her hair, pulled on bright cotton pants and a nicer-than-usual blouse, and rushed over to the kitchen. Rob was there ahead of her.

"No electricity," he muttered.

"What? You're kidding! No wonder my alarm didn't go off!"

"No, I'm not kidding. Fortunately, these are gas ovens. I turned the big one on to heat up the rolls."

Karen relaxed. "What would I do without your calm spirit?" she asked.

Rob grinned. "I don't know. The more important question is, what are we going to do for coffee?"

Karen gasped. "Oh, my! And that's especially important this morning." She ran over and peered into the top of the large coffee pot. Relieved, she said, "We still have yesterday's coffee. We could heat it up on the stove. With all the sugar they add, I doubt they'll even know it's left over."

"Good idea. And I think there are some candles in the back room for the tables. At least then they can see what they're eating!"

By the time the men arrived, the coffee had been heated, warm milk was waiting in pitchers, and breakfast was hot and ready. Two high school helpers had arrived, a little late, and carried the plates to the tables. With the candles lit, it looked as though the whole arrangement, candles and all, had been planned especially for their guests. The Venezuelan pastors murmured among themselves. As they ate heartily and came up to the counter for seconds, one of them asked Karen and Rob to come out to where the tables were. After doing so, the man said a few words in rapid Spanish, then all of the men clapped. Rob shook his head and laughed, then responded in Spanish. The men chuckled together as if it was a good joke.

"What are they saying?" asked Karen under her breath. "He spoke too fast for me to understand."

"They thanked us for our hospitality," he told Karen, "and they love the cinnamon rolls."

"Oh, good--but what was so funny?"

He looked over at her, a twinkle in his eye. "They thought that you were my wife."

She blushed in embarrassment, then the room resounded with applause as the lights suddenly came on. Relieved, Karen let out a sigh.

Preparing for that evening's hamburger barbecue with the additional attendees kept Karen and Rob both busy all day. Karen had even begged off Bible club, though she hated to. But with so many extra people, there was much work to be done. The maids baked fresh hamburger buns, made potato salad, and prepared a green salad and chocolate cake while Karen mixed spices into the burger and shaped patties. Rob mixed up some of his special barbecue sauce and made gallons and gallons of fruit drink. In-between preparation, lunch, consisting of leftovers, had to be heated up and served. For the pastors' conference, mid-morning and mid-afternoon snacks were prepared and delivered to the auditorium where the men were meeting.

"Whew!" By four-thirty Karen was exhausted. "After the picnic tonight, I'm going to crash!"

Rob gave her an understanding smile. "Me, too. Wanna crash together?"

The question came so unexpectedly Karen asked him to repeat it. "What?" she asked.

"Do you want to watch a movie or something after the picnic?" Rob asked. "When Pete's parents were here visiting, they told him about a couple new ones that just became available online. I thought you might like to watch something with me."

"Uh--" Karen faltered. Karen wasn't a big movie buff, but no matter--she would have watched anything with Rob regardless of how tired she was. She could feel her firm resolve flying out the window, and answered, "Sure. If I don't fall asleep before then!"

Rob gave her a heartwarming smile. "We're done here for now. Why don't you go take a nap, if you like."

"Well--what about loading the carts?"

"That can wait. I'm going to run get a quick shower. How 'bout if I meet you back here at five-thirty?"

"Ya know," Karen began, the notion warming in her. "That sounds like a great idea! I'll see you in an hour."

"Great. And don't forget our date," Rob added as Karen walked away, the words causing her heart to skip a beat. She smiled, remembering Rob's invitation to the church meeting when he had purposefully stated, "It's not really like a date." Tonight, he had bluntly said it was! Karen wondered at the difference in him but yawned and headed for her room.

An hour later Karen felt refreshed. She had napped for forty minutes, then quickly showered and put on fresh make-up. Punkin, as always wanting to help, jumped on her shoulders while she added blush. "I don't have time for you, sweetie," she told the kitty, setting it gently down on the bed. "But later on, Rob's coming over to get me, so be on your best behavior!" Karen wondered as she spoke if they would watch the movie in Rob's apartment or hers. Oh well, they could work out details later. The important thing was, they actually had a *date*.

Taking extra care with her appearance, Karen selected a bright pink T-shirt with pink and black print pants. The outfit would be plenty comfortable, and if the evening grew cool, she could wear the matching stretch top.

At precisely five-thirty, she headed back to the kitchen. Guided by the list, she began loading utensils, dishes, and food onto the cart. Rob breezed through the door five minutes later, whistling a happy tune. Karen looked up and smiled as he entered. His skin was pink from the hot shower, and his dark hair still wet.

"The fire's going good," he told her, brushing past her to help load the cart.

Karen was disappointed that he said nothing more personal to her as they pushed the cart and carried the rest of the food outside to the pit. But what had she expected? After all, it was only a "date". It wasn't like he had proposed marriage! Karen tried to hide her feelings and threw herself into making certain the evening's picnic went well. She arranged the serving table in orderly fashion as usual, setting plates first and silverware last, with food in-between. To help the line go more smoothly, Karen placed an open hamburger bun on each plate, then handed each person one as they walked by. As Rob cooked burger after burger, he piled them into the large metal pan to be dished up.

After several Venezuelan pastors had passed by, Karen noticed with a shock what each was doing. Since the bun was open and the meat was plentiful, the men were each taking two burgers the first time through. Karen gasped, then walked over to where Rob was flipping burgers. She explained the situation to him quietly. "Do we have enough burgers for them to do that?" she asked pointedly.

"Well, we may not by the time the last person gets through the line!" He grimaced. Then smiling nonchalantly, Rob added another cooked burger to the pile and handed the tongs to Karen. "Why don't you put one burger on the plate before handing the plate to them," he suggested. "Don't leave a fork or anything in the pile of burgers. They'll get the idea."

His calm assurance instantly relieved her anxiety. She did as he said, and by the time the first person came through for second helpings, she was pleased there were still burgers left. She shot Rob a grateful smile, which he returned.

Karen watched with interest as a grade-school girl heaped her plate high with wiggly red Jello. She was always amused at the food tastes of the different age groups. The little girls came back for seconds of fruit and Jello, the guys for meat, and the teenage girls for salad. Tonight was no exception.

"Enjoying the picnic?" she asked the child. The girl responded with a big grin, then hurried off with her ponytails bobbing.

Rob had filled a plate and gone to eat his meal, and she could see him laughing at a table with Pete and Amanda. As Karen began dishing up her own plate, he surprised her by coming up behind her.

"Say, Karen," he began, "uh--Pete wants to watch the movie with us tonight. Would you mind?"

Realizing she would no longer be alone with Rob, a wave of disappointment came over her. Feeling she had little choice, however, she readily agreed. "Uh--sure, that's fine," she faltered, though it really wasn't. "Should we use my apartment?"

"That'd be great," Rob answered, obviously relieved. "Pete's and my place is pretty much of a mess!"

Karen smiled. "I'm sure Punkin will enjoy all the company."

"You're a real sport, Karen," Rob said with a twinkle in his eye, and touched her arm gratefully. "I mean, it seemed rude to turn him down, and it IS his large-screen computer we'll be using."

"That's okay," Karen reassured him. "It'll be fun. And where Pete goes, Amanda goes, so I guess it's a double date! I've got some microwave popcorn my mom sent me, if anyone's still hungry after this feast!"

As soon as all the food was put away, Karen headed for her room. The picnic cleanup had not taken long--the only food left was a partial bowl of sliced pickles and a few carrot sticks. Karen remembered that, only hours earlier, the containers had all been full. She was glad they didn't have to serve that many people every week!

"Meow!" The kitten greeted her the minute she opened the door.

"Hi, Sweetie!" Karen scooped the little kitten up and gave it a warm squeeze. "Guess what, we're having company! Let's get this place cleaned up!"

There wasn't much to be done. Karen's apartment was rarely out of order since she spent so little time there. She took a quick look around and decided to center her attention on refreshments. Opening the fridge, she was pleased to note that there were a few diet sodas left. That was one amenity she had not given up for missionary life!

At the knock on the door minutes later, Karen, expecting to see Rob, was surprised to find Kelly standing in the hallway.

"Hi," Kelly greeted her pleasantly. "Is this where the movie is?"

"Uh--yes," Karen stammered. "I think I'd better get a couple more chairs." The sofa would hold three, then one in each armchair made five. She brought in the desk chair from her bedroom in case word of the movie spread.

"I think Cathy and Jennifer are coming, too," Kelly commented. "We're so starved for movies in English! What little time I do have I usually spend reading, but tonight I'm so tired I just want to let my brain relax. Oh," she squealed upon noticing Punkin, "your kitten is so cute!"

Karen smiled as Kelly picked up the kitten and began to stroke his fur. She didn't know Kelly very well and was still taking in the fact that there were two more uninvited guests coming as well. "Maybe I should bring in a couple chairs from the dining hall," she murmured. Thinking better of it, she brought in the two pillows off her bed, turned the pillowcases inside out, and dropped them on the floor in front of the sofa. By the time she had done so, Rob had arrived, with Pete and Amanda in tow. Cathy and Jennifer were not far behind, and soon the little apartment was filled with noise and laughter. Rob shot her a meaningful look and shrugged his shoulders. Karen only grinned back at him. While Rob set up the movie, Karen poured drinks for everyone who wanted them, then put a bag of microwave popcorn in to pop.

Jennifer was curious about her apartment and asked for a tour. Karen, pleased at their interest, showed the girls her bedroom and tiny bathroom.

"We have a bathtub," Amanda confided. "My favorite thing. I thought I was going to have to go all year without a bath!"

"Oooh," breathed Kelly, spying the women's magazine flipped open on Karen's bed. "Where EVER did you get this?"

Karen smiled. "From my mom. I got a goodie package the other day--stayed up half the night reading. Would you like to borrow it?"

"*Would* I? Do you know how much these cost here? *When* you can find them? The last one I saw was at the airport, for the equivalence of five dollars! Are you sure you're through with it, though?"

"I've read what I wanted to for now," she assured Kelly. "Go ahead."

"Can I have it after her?" asked Cathy. Karen laughed. "Sure. Just don't forget where you borrowed it from!"

By the time Rob was through setting up and they had agreed on what to watch, everyone but him and Karen had chosen a seat. The only places left were beside Pete and Amanda on the sofa, which was only room for one, and both pillows on the floor. Kelly had opted to stay in the bedroom to read the magazine. Karen sat down on the sofa beside the engaged couple, feeling a little like a third wheel in her own living room.

Rob asked, "Ready, everybody?" He started the movie and sat down cross-legged on the floor in front of Karen. As the movie began, she whispered to him, "Are you comfortable?"

"I'm fine," he whispered. "Just fine." Karen sat back in her seat and was soon absorbed in the movie. She became vaguely aware that Rob was leaning up against her legs, his head resting back against her knees.

As the hour grew late, Karen felt herself nodding off to sleep. Before she realized what was happening, she awoke to a gentle shaking of her shoulder. "Karen?" came a quiet, deep voice.

"What--huh?" Karen felt groggy but woke enough to stare into Rob's dark eyes.

"Boy, you weren't kidding when you said you'd fall asleep!" Rob teased.

Karen looked around, yawning as she did so. "Is the movie over? Where is everyone?"

"They left. They said 'thanks.'"

Karen became aware of Rob sitting next to her on the sofa, one arm draped around her, pulling her closer to him so that her head rested on his shoulder. She did not want the pleasant sensation to end but knew she should get up and go to bed.

"What time is it?" she asked sleepily.

"Twelve-thirty. The movie ended half an hour ago."

"What have you been doing for half an hour?" she asked, popping her head up as she did so.

Rob's hand gently eased her head back down, and Karen didn't resist. "Just enjoying having you in my arms," he said huskily, squeezing her shoulder. "Trying to salvage what's left of our date!" He gently kissed the top of her head.

Karen sighed a deep, happy sigh. The kitten, sleeping beside her, purred contentedly.

* * *

Karen sat thoughtfully chewing on the end of her pencil. She had been working on the same week's menu for half an hour and was running out of ideas. "Rob," she began, as he walked into the kitchen after his computer class, "has the school ever polled the students to see what their favorite foods are?"

Rob laid his notebook on the counter and pulled a stool up next to her. "Hmm. I don't know about 'ever', but it hasn't been done since I've been here. That's a good idea."

"I've been thinking," Karen continued, "after staring at this menu for over thirty minutes, I'm getting tired of pancakes for breakfast every tenth day or so. On the other hand, I know there are kids who would LOVE pancakes every day, and others who would choose cold cereal over just about anything."

Rob nodded. "And the guys seem to prefer the heartier meals, while the girls love it when we have baked potato bar, chef salad, stuff like that. And a little classier stuff, like Chicken Cordon Bleu for that one banquet, whereas the guys would be perfectly happy with fried chicken, biscuits and gravy!"

"Exactly!" Karen smiled. Unlike a lot of men she had known, including a few at her office, Rob always seemed to be on the same wavelength. He treated her as an equal, appreciated and encouraged her ideas, and respected her even when they had a difference of opinion.

"It's always been like that, though," Rob went on. "We can't please all of them all the time."

"I know, but it would sure be nice to please *most* of them *most* of the time!" Karen said.

"Yeah, I guess it would. Do you want me to draft something up on the computer? A survey, I mean?"

"Oh, that would be great! I've been writing down some thoughts. Can you help me?"

"Sure. Let me grab a cup of coffee first. Want one?"

"Love one, thanks," she replied, thinking how he was too good to be true. With five siblings, he had probably become used to helping out early in life. "With cream and sugar. Do you mind?"

" *Café con leche*, eh?" Rob grinned, knowing it was Karen's favorite. He poured a cup of black coffee for himself, then fixed Karen's and sat back down at the counter.

"Thanks." She sipped it gratefully. "First, I thought I would list all of the foods we normally serve. Maybe the kids could rate them on a one-to-ten scale."

"Uh huh," Rob agreed. "And we could pass it out at a meal if you like. Where they're relaxed and will really take time to answer our questions--probably supper."

The two worked amicably together on the survey for the next hour, until Karen decided she had better get ready to serve supper. Rob went to his classroom to type it up. Just before the kids filed in for the meal, he handed Karen a clean white draft. "What do you think?"

Karen scanned the sheet of paper. "It looks great! Do you want to pass it out tonight? It's raining--the kids won't be in a hurry to go shoot hoops or anything."

Rob shrugged. "I don't see why not. Maybe then you can finish that menu you've been working on!"

"Maybe!" Karen agreed.

Rob ran back to the school office to get pencils and make copies. Karen stood at the kitchen counter and dished up lasagna and green beans. When Rob returned, he took his place next to her at the counter. After everyone was seated, he walked out into the dining hall to make the announcement.

Two high schoolers passed out the papers, and the dining hall was filled with noisy conversation as the students answered the questions on the survey. Grade-schoolers eagerly scrawled their marks on the sheets of paper, pleased that their opinions mattered. High school boys loudly verbalized their "least favorite meal" as the girls laughed at their descriptions. Karen and Rob watched in amazement, and had the meal almost completely cleaned up before everyone had finished writing.

Karen had to laugh later that evening as she and Rob reviewed the survey results together. The two were in Karen's apartment, with completed surveys spread out on the glass coffee table. Rob sat in the wicker chair and Karen was curled up on the sofa.

"Shoo!" she scolded Punkin as the kitten for the third time jumped into the middle of the papers. She picked up the kitty and squeezed it, then kissed it on the top of the head. "Now go play," she ordered, setting him on the floor.

"Oh, would that bad behavior would get *me* so much negative attention," Rob teased, watching her with an unreadable look on his face, and Karen burst out laughing.

The rain continued to pour outside. Karen was grateful to be inside but was still a little chilly. She shivered, then excused herself to the bedroom to get a sweater.

"Now this is interesting," Rob commented as she re-entered the living room. "Pancakes is their all-time favorite! Here's what one person wrote: 'I especially liked them that day they were so light and fluffy they almost bubbled out of the pan.'"

"What? You're joking! No one *really* wrote that, did they?" She grabbed the paper out of Rob's hand and immediately recognized the handwriting. Karen giggled. "Wouldn't I know it. Roxie!"

"Pancakes *are* what they like best, though," Rob insisted. "Twenty-nine kids chose them as their favorite breakfast. Remember, that's over creamed eggs AND biscuits and gravy, though biscuits and gravy was a close second. And," he went on, "pancakes was the *least* favorite of six of the students!"

Karen shook her head. "Now I know why I get so frustrated trying to please everyone!"

Rob continued to scan the results. "I bet tacos will end up as number one supper," he predicted. "Especially with those homemade tortillas the maids make. Or else pepperoni pizza."

"I still can't believe *pabellón* is so well liked," Karen admitted. When she had first heard of the popular black beans and rice combination, she thought it was the grossest food she had ever heard of. "Too bland," she had told Rob, vowing never to place it on the menu.

Rob had challenged her. "You watch and see. The meat and seasoning bring it all together. It's always a hit with the kids."

And it was. They came back for seconds and thirds. The maids added a special seasoning that brought out the flavor of both the beans and the rice. Since then, it had become one of Karen's favorites as well.

"Yeah, looks like it gets fifth place for supper fare," said Rob. Together they finished tabulating the figures and compiled the results, which they agreed to post the next morning at breakfast. Then Rob helped Karen finish the following week's menu based on their findings.

"Oooh, it's late," Karen noted, glancing at her watch. "I'm kind of a night owl, but it's hard when we have to get up so early!"

"Yeah, I really should be going," Rob agreed, then grinned at her playfully. "After all, I wouldn't want to ruin your reputation or anything."

"No problem--I have men in quite regularly until at least midnight or later," Karen boasted, her eyes twinkling.

"Oh--yeah?" Rob's eyes challenged. Karen was painfully aware that they were alone in her apartment after eleven o'clock on a weekday. The junior girls upstairs had gone to bed hours ago, and Joe and Roxie were probably getting ready for bed themselves. It was becoming increasingly more difficult to be alone with Rob so much and not give in to the strong physical attraction she felt for him.

Rob rose from his chair as if to leave, then surprised her by turning serious. "Ya know, I've always hesitated at spending this much time with any *one* single woman at the school."

"Oh? Why is that?"

"Well, you know, everyone at the school sees each other all the time, spends as much time together as any married couple. What if I went with one woman for a while, then broke it off? Then I've got one that hates me, and with a woman it's never just one, since she usually has a roommate or a friend as well. Talk about narrowing the field!"

Karen threw back her head and laughed.

"Anyway--truthfully, I've felt that it's just best to treat them all as sisters. I have dated occasionally, like taking Kelly to the banquet, but I've tried never to show favoritism to any of them."

Karen wondered what he was getting at. She was still seated and glanced up at Rob with a question in her eyes.

His voice grew quieter. "Until you." He reached down with both hands and gently pulled her to her feet. "Do you mind?"

She was uncertain which question she was answering. Did she mind the favoritism? Him spending so much time with her? Or being pulled to her feet? Right now, it was 'no' to everything. How could she possibly mind anything Rob did? He was her friend, but more than that. He had seen her through times of loneliness and sickness, overlooked her inadequacies in the kitchen and forgiven her mistakes, encouraged her ideas and experiments. Her head was telling her not to fall in love with him; her heart already had. But what would happen in June when they went their separate ways?

Aware that there was still a question in the air, Karen's heart pounded. She stood facing him and said quietly, "No, I don't mind." It wasn't exactly a declaration of love, but the words seemed to be what Rob wanted to hear.

Though a kiss would have been nice, Rob had other ideas. He pulled Karen to him and held her close for a few minutes, as though he did not want to let her go. Finally, he released her, said "good night" and walked through her door.

Karen sighed. *Men.* Who could figure them? They should come with instruction manuals.

One afternoon a few weeks later, Karen was standing at the counter wrapping aluminum foil around burger, carrots, potatoes and onion for a class campout when Paul Birch approached her.

"Karen, would you consider staying on another year?" he asked point blank. The question caught Karen completely off guard. She was hot and tired, and her feet ached from standing on the hard tile floor most of the day.

"Another year?" she repeated.

"Yes. There was a woman who had planned to come--she's been at language school. But she has severe health problems, and the doctors say she needs to stay in the States."

Karen felt like crying. "But, I--"

"You don't have to answer me now," he reassured her. "I know it's been hard for you. But sometimes, after people get used to being here, they decide this is where they'd like to stay. At least for a second year. So, I just wondered...if you'd at least pray about it." Paul Birch was not often without words, but his hesitancy told Karen he had thought a lot about it before approaching her.

Karen nodded. "Okay, I'll pray about it."

She tried to give the matter serious thought. Even though she looked forward to the end of the year when she could pack up her bags and leave, each day brought her heart a little closer to this country and the people who lived here. And Rob.... But now Rob was out of the picture as far as South America was concerned. He had previously planned to stay on but was just offered a job in the States. He was, in his words, a "software expert," a skill which was in great demand. When she returned to her new job in Seattle, they would only be two thousand miles apart, not two continents.

But her decision could not involve him. If God wanted her in South America, she would stay, but certainly He would not make her stay now. Not NOW! She would go home, and she would take that new position as office manager. Her future was set.

It would have been simpler just to tell Mr. Birch "No". But she had promised to pray, so during the next few days she prayed. And pondered. And brooded.

Not usually so moody, Karen knew Rob was concerned about her. "Are you okay?" he asked at one point.

"I'm fine. Just thinking."

The maids had just removed large baking trays of oatmeal cookies from the oven. "Hmmmm," Karen murmured. "*Mi favorito*."

The maids laughed, and Karen joined in. Last week she had said sugar cookies were her favorite, and before that it was peanut butter. Having been in an apartment all by herself in Seattle and rarely actually cooking, the freshly baked goodies were always a treat. Mindful of her weight, she stopped at one and helped herself to a second cup of coffee.

Rob glanced at her anxiously but seemed glad to see her smiling. Karen was grateful he did not push the issue, as she was not ready to discuss the matter with anyone. It was between her and God.

They both suddenly became aware of a commotion out front, and of Yogi's insistent bark.

"Oh, what now?" Rob groaned. Curious, Karen followed him as he walked to the front double doors and opened them.

What greeted them was a curious sight. The little man they had hired to sharpen knives was back but could not enter the building because of Yogi's guard.

Yogi sat growling as the man stood quietly in fear. At once he straightened and made the motion of crossing his heart with his hand. Karen almost burst out laughing, but because of the man's fear she only smiled inwardly.

Rob spoke to the man in rapid Spanish. The man shrugged and began to answer, as Karen petted Yogi and tried to quiet him. Rob was shaking his head and telling the man, "No," and then words Karen did not understand. The man held up his hands as if giving up, then walked slowly away. Yogi stopped growling and began to lick Karen's hand.

"What was that all about?" she asked.

"He was drunk," Rob answered. "I don't mind hiring him, but in his present state I doubt the knives would get very sharp or that it would even be a safe thing for him to do!" He chuckled, shaking his head. "Did you see him crossing Yogi, like he was a priest or something?"

Karen chuckled. "Yeah. Well, I'd better get back to the kitchen. Roxie's coming by to pick me up in half an hour."

Roxie, in keeping her earlier promise to Karen, had already scoped out the town to see what was available in the way of schools for Pedro. Together they visited every grade school they knew of, none of which had the time or resources to deal with a deaf child. Karen, feeling defeated, had just about given up hope.

A few weeks after their search, a local Venezuelan pastor visited the school. He had long been a friend of Paul Birch and Paul had invited him to lunch in the dining hall when the Pastor and his wife dropped by for a visit. As the Venezuelan pastor walked by the counter, Rob asked the man's wife if she would care for salad, and she made no reply. Her husband made hand signs to her, and the woman smiled and nodded to Rob.

Karen's heart skipped a beat, and a chill ran down her spine. She and Rob exchanged glances, and he seemed to know what she was thinking. "Okay," he said after the couple had passed, "let's go talk to them." After the last person was served, they walked over to the pastor's table and introduced themselves. Rob and the couple, also with the help of sign language, had an animated conversation in Spanish, and Rob turned to Karen with a wide smile on his face.

"Karen, you won't believe this--she teaches right here in Rubio!"

"Oh! Where?"

Rob learned from the woman that there was one school that could help deaf students--not a regular grade school but a school for special needs children. They not only taught the deaf, but mentally and physically handicapped, as well.

"Could she teach Pedro how to read?" Karen asked.

Again, they discussed the matter. Karen waited.

"She doesn't see why not," Rob told her. "She'd like you to come by tomorrow morning, around ten, with Pedro. She will meet you then. Will his parents agree to it?"

"Yes!" Karen practically shouted. "Oh, yes!"

"Now don't get your hopes up," Rob advised. "I know you're excited, but there's always a chance there are other reasons he's not in school."

"I know," Karen admitted. "But at least I will have tried. I can't go back to Seattle without doing everything I possibly can to help him." Rob's eyes suddenly darkened, then he nodded and said, "Okay. I can drive you if you want. We'll go right after breakfast."

Early the next morning Rob drove her up the winding mountainside to talk to Pedro's mother. The woman clapped both hands over her face. "*Ay, Dios!*" She was obviously grateful, and Rob tried to explain to her that this was just preliminary, that there might be some reason it wouldn't work. Pedro, obviously excited as well, climbed into the jeep after his mother cleaned him up. She had work to do, she explained, and would wait for them, and pray.

"Not a bad idea," said Rob solemnly. He took Karen's hand, bowed his head, and asked that God would take care of Pedro and make a place for him at the school.

The meeting with the teacher went well. Pedro, eager to please, did exactly as he was told. The school nurse examined him and found that he could hear sounds but not words. Karen recalled how Pedro had always enjoyed the Bible songs and would clap to the music. She thought it was because the rest of them clapped, and he wanted to be like them. After the teacher met with Pedro, she pulled Karen aside.

"Yes?" Karen waited. Rob stood nearby to translate. Since the woman read lips, they conversed with little problem. But now Karen was nervous. What would they say?

The woman smiled. She began to slowly talk to Rob and when they were finished, Karen looked over at Rob anxiously.

"They can take him," he said, slowly letting out his breath. "But there's one problem."

Karen held her breath. "What?"

"Money. He would need to buy a school uniform. And the school has a minimal charge, which includes feeding him a morning snack, with milk. And he would need to pay for transportation down from the mountain every day."

Karen couldn't stop smiling. "That's not a problem! I'll find the money!" She looked over at the teacher. "*Oh, gracias, gracias! Muchas gracias!*"

The woman laughed. Rob took Karen's hand and led her outside. He explained that as soon as they bought Pedro the uniform--blue shorts and a white shirt--the mother could enroll him in school.

Karen was elated. She gave Pedro a big hug, and impulsively, she gave Rob a hug as well. Pedro seemed excited, and Karen asked Rob to explain things. Pedro just kept nodding. Karen had no idea if he understood at all but was certain he was enjoying the adventure.

The next week kept her busy working out the other details. Pedro's mother and father were in full support, and believed it was an answer from God. Rob and Karen took Pedro and his mother downtown to buy Pedro a uniform. Roxie arranged with a taxi driver picking up other children to take Pedro to school every morning and home again every afternoon.

"*Pero--el dinero,*" the mother had shrugged helplessly.

"The money," Roxie told her. "Where will she get the money? She knows you'll be leaving soon."

"I'll send it," Karen told Roxie. "Tell her I'll send it every month. You can count on it. I'll send it to you, Roxie. Okay?"

Roxie nodded and translated Karen's words. The mother was so grateful she had tears in her eyes. Now her son would get the same education as his brothers and sisters. She thanked them both, and Roxie reminded Carmelina to thank God in her prayers.

Karen was greatly relieved. Now she could go home knowing Pedro would be cared for.

At club the following week, Pedro seemed to have an extra shine about him. His little face beamed at her as she sang from her heart, "*Yo tengo gosa, gosa, gosa,*

gosa, en mi corazon...." Karen *did* have the joy, joy, joy, down in her heart. Her own happiness was mirrored in the smiles of the children around her. But as she clasped their hands and everyone swung around in a circle, she thought sadly of leaving them in a few short weeks. Who would visit them when she left for the States?

Karen wondered if anyone could visibly see the struggle that was going on inside of her. Did the pain show on her face? She had known many sleepless nights and restless days.

"Dear God," she prayed, tears streaming down her cheeks. "Let me be willing to stay, I can honestly pray that much. You know I don't want to stay, but please, bring me to the point where I'm willing to do your will, no matter what."

That prayer seemed to be the balm that soothed her frustrated soul. At last, the peace she had longed for filled her being, and she climbed into bed and drifted peacefully off to sleep.

CHAPTER TWELVE
Final Decisions

The year was too quickly drawing to a close. Graduation was three weeks away, and there was much to be done to accommodate the parents who would be visiting the school. Karen offered to help Grandma sew new drapes for the dining hall, so between Bible club, Spanish class, exercise class, and running the kitchen, she spent little time in her apartment. Out of guilt at neglecting Punkin, Karen brought him home some leftover chicken skin one evening. When he did not respond to her first call, she tried again. "Punkin!" She searched under the bed, on top of the curtain rod where he liked to climb, in the closet and behind the refrigerator. The kitten was nowhere to be found.

By this time, she was frantic. "Punkin!" She ran out into the hall, encountering Roxie's husband Joe. "Joe, he's gone!" she wailed.

"Who's gone?"

"Punkin! My kitty!"

Joe suggested they search the entire building. "I don't think he'd go outside with Yogi right there. Did you try the laundry room?" They split up and looked in every room. All of a sudden, Karen heard Joe laughing and went running back down the hall.

Joe was in the kitchen pantry, and there, behind several large containers, was the kitten. He was chomping noisily on a large black cockroach, which was hanging out either side of his mouth.

"Oh, Punkin!" Karen wanted to grab him and cuddle, but the idea of snuggling up to a cockroach was less than appealing. She shook her head and laughed in relief. "The poor little guy's been so cooped up! Or maybe he just doesn't like what I've been feeding him! Probably snuck out when I came over earlier and had the door open a few minutes.

"Thanks, Joe!" Very much relieved, she picked up her kitten, cockroach and all, and carried him back to the apartment.

Karen was relaxing on the sofa later that evening when she heard a timid knock at the door. Setting down the book she was reading, she opened the door to find two of Roxie's girls standing there, both looking anxious.

"Maria, Fabiola--hi! Can I help you with something?"

Maria's dark curls bobbed up and down as Fabiola responded in a rush of words. "Hi Aunt Karen, we're on a scavenger hunt and we still have two things left."

"Oh! What are they?"

"Hmmmm." Fabiola scanned the piece of paper in her hand. "A dead cockroach and a broken needle. Do you have either one?"

"A dead cockroach, indeed! Shucks, I had one earlier today but didn't think to save it!" Karen laughed. "Who thought up this list, anyway?"

Maria frowned. "Gross, huh? Our teacher did. And we have to have ALL the items on the list or we won't win a prize!"

"Can you help us?" begged Fabiola.

"Well...I don't keep too many dead bugs around, but I might be able to help you with the needle. Just a minute." Karen walked into the bedroom and looked into her sewing kit. She returned with a threaded needle. "Here's one, but it's not broken. Is it cheating if I break the needle myself?"

The girls shook their heads. "No, but we have to bring back a broken one. Can you break it, please?"

For the new few minutes, the girls watched as Karen stomped on the needle with her foot, but the needle stubbornly stayed in one piece. Finally, in desperation, she stuck a pencil just under the needle, and, when stepped on, it broke into two pieces.

"Yeah!" The girls snatched it up. "Thanks, Aunt Karen!" they called out as they scurried down the hall.

Karen laughed. "You're welcome! Let me know if you win!" Picking up her book, she shook her head. She would miss those girls. She would miss a lot of things.

Graduation day was fast approaching. The seniors, excited to take the next step in life but sad at leaving each other, spent many hours together. Karen began to realize that she, too, would soon be separated from many people she had come to love throughout the past nine months. She didn't even want to *think* about saying goodbye to Rob. Or Roxie. And what would she do with her little kitten? Her eyes misted at the thought.

With only two weeks to go, Karen was adjusting her meal plans accordingly. While still striving for good, fresh, attractive meals, she was also trying to use up leftovers and purchase only for the remaining fourteen days. The school would be empty all summer, and excess food would only spoil.

After supper one evening while she and Rob were putting food away, he pulled her aside. "Karen, I need to talk to you," he said in a serious tone. Karen had noticed he'd been quiet all day. She had tried to joke him out of it, but his introspection only seemed to deepen. Since he was normally so pleasant and good-natured, Karen was puzzled at his moodiness.

"Okay. Let me just take off my apron," she told him. Wiping her hands on a towel, she headed out of the kitchen. Together they walked out of the dining hall and into the night. The air was balmy, and she could hear the night frogs in the distance. Happy sounds of girls laughing and talking drifted out from the upstairs girls' dorm.

"Let's walk," Rob said stiffly. They walked companionably side by side along the sidewalk for a few blocks. Karen waited for him to break the silence. Suddenly he reached over and took her hand but kept walking.

"I responded to the job offer yesterday," he said, not looking at her. "Regarding the software position. The computer company in Colorado."

It wasn't like him to talk in monosyllables.

"Hmm hmm," she prompted. "Isn't that where you're from? Colorado?"

"Yes." He seemed nervous. "I had written to several places, uncertain whether God wanted me to stay on here or not."

"Uh huh." She waited for him to continue.

"Well, anyway, this is a great opportunity. Good pay, great benefits. Nice future. Everything I could have asked for."

"I know. I'm very happy for you," she said sincerely. She *was* very happy for him, even though it meant they would be at different ends of the earth.

He took a deep breath and stopped walking. "Yeah, but--Karen, it's tearing me up inside to tell you this, but--I've turned down the offer. I'm going to stay on here."

Karen's heart stopped.

"Well, anyway, I just thought you should know." Rob looked at the ground and bit his lip nervously. He dropped Karen's hand and stuffed both of his own into his pockets.

Karen caught her breath. She and Rob had never actually dated, or even discussed their feelings for one another. But somehow, she always saw him in her future. And now God was bringing them together, independent of one another.

Only yesterday had she made her own choice. They had *both* made their decisions, knowing that those decisions could take them to two different continents.

She touched him lightly on the shoulder, and he turned to face her. "Rob, I--I don't know how to tell you this." Her eyes filled with tears.

"Tell me what?"

She smiled and looked warmly into the eyes of the man she loved. "They've asked me to stay on another year too, and--I've accepted. God won."

A slow smile spread over Rob's entire face. He let out a loud "Whoop!" and grabbed her in a big bear hug. They both began talking at once, with Karen trying to tell him she thought he'd taken the offer in the States and Rob trying to tell Karen he thought she was going home. They both laughed, and Rob pulled her tightly to him.

"You mean, you finally feel like you belong here?" Rob whispered, his face nuzzled against her ear.

"Yes, Rob," she said softly, "I belong right here, with you."

Rob's eyes watered. He released his hold on her, then cupped her face with his hands and kissed her tenderly on the lips for the very first time. The kiss held promise, of tomorrows together working side by side. Of God's best for both of them.

This was truly a land of promise.

Author Bio:

My first published work was a mini-mystery for Woman's World magazine. I have written numerous short stories, including a true experience of helping a homeless couple which was published in a Sunday School paper. Writing has been my passion since childhood -- but as life intervened and other priorities bullied their way, it was forced to take a back seat in my life. Attending an OCW Summer Conference was a giant BOOST for jumping back into the front seat of the writing world. I primarily write inspirational romance and mystery but very much enjoy interviews. In years past I did an interview of a church lady for every issue of the women's newsletter at church. I am currently working on marketing my four novels (three inspirational romance, one mystery).

My first husband and I fostered many children and were active in youth group and camps. After 10 years of marriage, we spent a year in Venezuela as head cooks at a school for missionary children. My husband passed away in 2016, and I continued working full-time for a law firm until retirement in 2020. In 2021, I rekindled a teenage friendship and married the Executive Director of a network of Baptist churches (in essence, a pastor). Now I enjoy spending time traveling with him, transcribing court hearings, and writing.